# LESSONS IN LOVE

A SEXY SINGLE DAD WESTERN ROMANCE

COWBOYS OF LONG VALLEY ROMANCE
BOOK EIGHT

ERIN WRIGHT

# CHAPTER I

## ELIJAH

August, 2018

THE SUN WAS JUST peeking over the horizon, sending bright rays of light straight into Elijah's eyeballs. He blinked and then scrubbed at his eyes with the heels of his hands, trying to push the burning pain away.

So. Damn. Exhausted. He was gonna go home and sleep for a week. Maybe two.

Ah hell, who was he kidding. He was gonna go home to try to sleep during the day – which never worked, not real well, anyway – and then he was gonna go on back to Mr. Petrol's that night and start this hellish nightmare called his job all over again.

He yawned so hard his jaw cracked, and he rubbed at his eyes again, then began slapping his cheeks lightly. He just had to stay awake for a few more minutes. He didn't live real far away from Mr. Petrol's, thank God. He could…

*What the hell?*

He pulled off into the Cleveland Elementary School parking lot and stared up at their reader board.

OPEN - FT JANITOR POSITION W/ BENN. APPLY INSIDE.

Suddenly, he felt a lot more awake.

Like, a *whole* lot more awake.

"A position at the elementary school," he said softly to himself, and then began to laugh a little. "A position at the elementary school. Oh, what would Sarah have to say about that!"

He jumped out of his older-than-dirt truck, slamming the driver's side door closed as he gleefully hurried up the sidewalk towards the admin office. He'd dropped Brooksy off enough at school that he knew just where to go.

*Hot damn! A full-time job with benefits, during the day, right here in Sawyer, Idaho. I don't give a rat's ass if I have to scrub toilets with a toothbrush – I'll do it!*

This – this was what he'd been looking for, for months now. But with his smarts and skills…no one had wanted him.

He shoved that thought away. He didn't need to be a college graduate or even a smart guy to push a broom around. Which was damn good, since he wasn't either.

"Can I help you?" Mrs. Worsop asked over her half-moon glasses, looking up at him from behind her giant wooden desk. She'd been the secretary for the school since he was a kid, and from what he could remember, she'd been old back then. Did she have some sort of secret stash of the Fountain of Life hidden away in that desk of hers? Nothing else explained how she could stay ancient – but not die – for decades at a time. "Are you here to register Brooklyn for school?"

The elderly woman was craning her wrinkled neck, trying to peer around him as if he was suddenly gonna pull his ten-year-old daughter out of his back pocket like some sort of elaborate magic trick.

"No, I'm not here for that. I'm here about the janitor job. Has it been filled yet?"

Honest to God, just asking the question terrified him a little.

It'd be just his luck to find out about the position right after they'd gone and hired somebody else. He hadn't seen anything on the board out front about it before today, but then again, he couldn't rightly say that he paid much attention to the shit they put up.

"The…the janitor job?" the secretary echoed faintly, staring at him in disbelief. "And just how long have you been harboring a deep-seated desire to clean toilets, Mr. Morland?"

"It's always been something I've wanted to do, actually," he said with a straight face. "Forever," he added.

*Please, please, please.*

He'd get down on one knee and beg if that's what they were wanting. He wouldn't like it, but he'd do it.

Mrs. Worsop just stared at him, one eyebrow arched, waiting for him to crack and tell her the truth.

He just stared back, not blinking.

*Anything for Brooksy. Anything at all.*

"Well," the older lady finally sniffed when the silence became so awkward, people a block away were probably feeling antsy and didn't even know why, "the interviews are tomorrow morning. Here's the application." She pulled a double-sided piece of paper out of a cabinet drawer and handed it over to him. "You just fill that out and come on back. Eight in the morning is when they start."

He took the paper and thanked her properly, scanning it as he headed back towards his truck. Now all he had to do was figure out how to sell the principal on the idea that he'd never wanted anything as much as he wanted to mop and wax floors.

*If I'm there in the classroom with Brooksy, cleaning it…well, there's not a damn thing Sarah can say about it. It's not like she can demand I quit my job that's paying for the child support, right?*

Elated, he did a fist pump in the air. *Hells* to the yes. He didn't consider himself to be a real smart man, but at that moment, he was king of the world.

# CHAPTER 2

## HANNAH

HANNAH LAMBERT LOOKED over the class roll for the year, double-checking that each child on the list had been assigned a desk on the seating chart. The names of Dayton and Tahlia caught her eye – they were both younger siblings to students she'd had in the past. It was always fascinating to see the differences between siblings. Was Dayton going to be a hellion like his older brother had been? It could be an...*interesting* school year if Dayton was even vaguely like his brother.

*Speaking of hellions...*

Her eyes stopped on the name of Brooklyn Morland. Just yesterday in the teacher's lounge, the teachers had been gossiping about who was getting which student, and Brooklyn's fourth grade teacher, Mr. Pettengill, had asked who'd been "stuck with that Morland girl" this year. Hannah's neck had flushed red with anger at his tone, and she'd been debating if she could get away with saying nothing at all when another teacher had ever-so-helpfully piped up and informed everyone that Hannah had her this year.

*Thank you, Betsy. Really, you're awesome.*

Every eye in the teacher's lounge had swung towards her,

pinning her to her chair. Even now, a day later, she felt herself covered with goosebumps just remembering the ordeal. Despite having worked at the Cleveland Elementary School for the past twelve years, the idea of speaking in front of a group of adults…

Terrifying.

So, of course, she hadn't said a word; she'd just smiled a little at the group as she'd died inside.

No, worse. She *hadn't* died – inside or out – which meant that she then had to listen as Mr. Pettengill began detailing Brooklyn's fall from grace. Oh, she'd been such a "sweet young thang" when she'd started the fourth grade, but she'd quickly turned into a beast and he'd had to keep a firm hand with her.

Which was, of course, when Mr. Pettengill began lecturing Hannah on how to take care of an unruly child like Brooklyn; to make sure that she knew from Day One that Hannah was watching her and would punish her for the tiniest of infractions.

Which was when her soul shriveled into a tiny ball.

There were days – like, 365 of them a year – where Mr. Pettengill resembled a boot camp instructor more than a fourth grade teacher.

Finally – *fin-a-lly* – the conversation turned to gossip about other students, and the focus moved off Hannah, which meant she could breathe normally again. Honestly, if she'd had any idea how much she'd need to interact with adults as a teacher, she probably would've picked another profession. Maybe she could've been a deep sea diver where all she would have to interact with were sharks.

Sharks were honestly preferable to Mr. Pettengill, and didn't *that* just about say it all.

She heard a knock on the door of her classroom, yanking her back to the present. "Come in," she called out, absentmindedly pushing her glasses back up the bridge of her nose and looking to see who was there.

*Mylanta!*

As if thinking about the daughter had conjured up the father, there stood Mr. Morland in the doorway, his slim frame bulging with just enough muscles to make a girl drool.

*'Just enough muscles to make a girl drool?' Where did that come from?*

She shot to her feet, her chair skittering backwards and slamming into the painted cinder-block wall behind her. A deep red blush started at her toes and quickly worked its way up her body, staining her cheeks a flaming red she was just sure could be seen from outer space. Some satellite was probably being steered off course right now by the sheer luminescence of her cheeks.

"Hello, Mr. Morland," she said formally, trying to ignore the state of her cheeks and the fact that her darn chair was still sliding, ever so slowly, along the wall.

*Stop rolling. Any day now. You can stop moving. Really, you can.*

Mr. Morland walked in, his dark eyes tracking the progress of the errant chair, and then he turned them back towards her, and she was pinned into place yet again. They were this fascinating gray-green color that she'd never seen before; cool, aloof, but just a hint of something more beneath that.

"Hello, Miss Lambert," he replied just as formally as her, pulling on the brim of his cap. Her chair, thank the Lord above, had finally come to a stop. Hannah could just see it out of the corner of her eye, listing to the side drunkenly. She really needed to buy a new one, but that meant not buying any classroom supplies for the year and if she had to choose between a nice chair for her or pencils and markers for her students…

Drunken chair it was.

"Are you…" She cleared her throat, trying to get the croak out of it. Adults were just tall children, she reminded herself.

Very tall, very handsome children.

Hmmmm…actually, not *too* tall – the perfect height, really, especially for a person of short stature like her.

Okay, so that wasn't helping.

"Are you…are you here to talk about Brooklyn?" she finally got out. She scrambled inwardly as she talked, trying to remember how old he was in relation to her, and made the vague guess that he was three years younger, maybe four.

A younger man…she didn't *do* younger men.

Ever.

Something her libido was apparently choosing in that very moment to forget.

"Oh!" he said, his brow wrinkled in surprise. "No, actually, I didn't realize she was gonna be in your class this year. My ex was the one who signed her up for school. I'm the new janitor here now that Mr. Longspee's retired, so I just wanted to say howdy to everyone and let y'all know that I'm gonna be the one cleaning in here."

As he spoke, his rich voice with a hint of a drawl sent sparks up her arms. She scrubbed at them and then held them against her chest, hugging herself. Anxious to give herself something to do – anything that didn't involve looking Mr. Morland in the eye, that was – she hurried over and began tugging her errant chair back towards her desk. "Well, welcome," she said over her shoulder, concentrating fully on the listing chair. She didn't actually need to use every bit of concentration on the task but she wanted to, since the chair was a lot safer than Mr. Morland was.

Considering how her body felt on fire at that moment, nuclear explosions seemed safer than Mr. Morland.

Which was patently ridiculous. He'd graduated from Sawyer a handful of years after her, so she'd seen him occasionally at pep rallies, the grocery store, a football game…

But she'd never felt like this before. Not that she'd disliked him; it just hadn't occurred to her *to* like him.

Until today, that was. Suddenly, her body and libido were all sorts of awake and paying attention.

*Now?! Right now you choose to sit up and drool?!*

A couple of months ago, when Mr. Kiener had asked her out for coffee, all her libido had done was curl up in the corner and take a nap. It didn't help that he was 20 years her senior and missing some of his teeth. He was a nice enough guy; a widower looking for someone to cook for him now that his wife was gone.

Yeah, her libido had taken a real long snooze that day.

"Is there anything I need to work on or do for you here in your classroom?" Mr. Morland asked. He was busy looking around the room, apparently searching for a project to tackle, and she tried to control the panic flooding through her at the thought of him spending lots of time in her classroom, doing things.

Anything at all.

Like, breathing or something.

"No," she squeaked, and then cleared her throat, shoving her glasses back up the bridge of her nose. "No, we're ready for the new year. Thank you, though." She was so formal, her back so rigid, she would've been right at home in one of those atrocious whale-boned corsets women wore in the 1800s.

She knew she was being dumb.

She knew that this gut reaction to his presence was ridiculous.

1. She was an old maid;
2. She was never getting married – everyone knew that;
3. He was a younger man;
4. He was apparently now her coworker; and
5. He was the father of one of her students.

She couldn't have special ordered someone to be less suitable for her.

Too bad her twisting, turning, trembling stomach didn't agree.

Mr. Morland pulled on the bill of his ball cap, murmured,

"Have a good one," and then was gone. On his way to go torture another teacher with his muscles and eyes and tight butt.

Okay, so maybe Mr. Pettengill wasn't exactly panting over Mr. Morland's gray-green eyes and tight butt, which was not fair, honestly. Why did they have to affect *her* like this?

Hannah collapsed into her chair and stared at the empty doorway.

She was in trouble, all right.

# CHAPTER 3

## ELIJAH

SEPTEMBER, 2018

" I CHECKED MY ACCOUNT," Sarah slurred, clearly already most of the way through a bottle of wine, "and there ain't nothin' in there yet."

Elijah clenched his jaw so tight, he was a little worried it'd take an act of God to pull it apart again. "I already told you this'd happen," he ground out. "There's a gap between my last paycheck at Mr. Petrol's, and my first paycheck at the school district. I'm gonna be two weeks late. I told you about this when I got the job at the school."

"But how am I shupposed to pay my bills?" she whined. "I need zhat money." He heard her taking a loud slurp of what was undoubtedly more wine, even as her words ran together so much, he almost couldn't understand her.

The thing was, she didn't need his money. Not really. With the money she'd inherited after her parents had died in that godawful car wreck, she was pretty much set for life. It was why she'd finally told him to go screw himself; that she was gonna divorce him. She didn't need to pretend to love him anymore, as she so bluntly put it, just so she could stay married to him and live off his income. She was a rich woman now.

A-yup, after about two days of genuine mourning for her parents, her tears dried right up when she realized how rich she was about to be.

So no, she didn't need his child support payment each month. She loved making him pay it, knowing it made his life just that much more difficult to afford, but she didn't *need* it.

The truth was, she was pissed 'cause he'd done the run-around on her. He'd figured out how to see their daughter without getting permission from the courts beforehand, and if there was one thing Sarah hated, it was losing. It wasn't that she loved their daughter that much – she wasn't capable of it – but she hated not coming out on top, no matter what.

"Sarah," he growled, his temper dangerously close to snapping, "you'll be paid in full just as soon as—"

"If your child support payment is 21 days and two minutes overdue, I'll sic the sheriff on you," she cut in, and then hung up.

Elijah slammed his hand down on the table, scaring Brooklyn's pet hamster into scurrying into the corner of his cage and hiding.

"Dammit!" Elijah roared at the world. He'd been so sure he'd outsmarted Sarah for once, but here she was with the upper hand again. After he'd been hired at the school district, he'd sat down and calculated pay periods, and had known then that he was up shit creek without a paddle. He was gonna have to rely on Sarah's goodwill not to get into trouble over this.

And relying on Sarah's goodwill was never a good idea.

He was stupid, too stupid. He was never gonna be like his brother Aaron. He wasn't the golden child. He wasn't the educated child. He wasn't the pillar of the community. No matter how hard he tried or what he did, he was a failure in everyone's eyes, including his own.

He shouldn't have tried to beat Sarah at her own game. That was a huge mistake right there. She was the one with the smarts, who could out-think everyone else and force 'em to do what she wanted 'em to do. Their 10-year marriage was proof of that. Beating Sarah at her own game was a fool's dream.

And in this, he was certainly the fool.

# CHAPTER 4
## HANNAH

AMELIA, HANNAH'S AIDE, circulated around the classroom, helping keep an eye on the students as they started in on their bell work for the day. It was three weeks into the school year and the students were just beginning to settle in, having spent those three weeks testing Hannah's boundaries, Amelia's boundaries, and no doubt the school secretary's boundaries, just to see where they were at.

Hannah had known to expect it, of course – it was just the way fifth graders operated. Old enough to test boundaries; young enough to respect them once they found them. It was one of the reasons why Hannah loved this age so much. Too young, and they'd want her to wipe their nose for them. Too old, and they'd be too cool to listen to a teacher.

Yeah, fifth graders were just about right.

Hannah had finished another elaborate coloring page last night, this one of a frog drawn in mid-jump, and she was taking advantage of the quiet, focused nature of the students to hang the finished product up above their in-class terrarium. She stepped down from the chair and looked up at the high-quality coloring page with a pleased smile.

It'd taken her two weeks to get both the shading of the water and the sun on the frog's skin just right. She couldn't draw a stick figure to save her life, but she sure could color. She didn't brag, of course, but if forced into a corner, she'd name coloring, riding horses, and teaching as being her (only) talents in life.

Luckily for her, two of those talents went hand-in-hand. The cinder block walls of her classroom had long ago been painted an ugly tan that had since turned a nasty dull gray, and without any decorations to brighten things up, she would end up in the insane asylum by the end of the school year, no doubt about it. In an attempt to make her classroom appear less like a federal prison and more like an elementary classroom, she'd begun decorating it with coloring pages depicting every animal and flower and scenic view a soul could imagine, using the bright colors and beauty to bring a liveliness to her room that would otherwise be lacking.

She even had a student's corner where her kids could bring in pages they'd colored, to show off to their classmates, and that board tended to be one of the most popular in the classroom. Even the shyest and most introverted of students could brag on that board, something Hannah was especially proud of. Too many school activities only rewarded the outgoing and/or athletic students. What about the Hannahs of the world? Making a difference to those students was what kept her going every day.

Newest coloring page hung up, Hannah turned and began scanning the room automatically, checking for problems or students wanting help. Everything looked fine – that was, until she spotted Brooklyn raising her head from her paper to look around furtively.

Yet another reason to love fifth graders: They were too young and innocent to be good at being sneaky. Brooklyn was about to do something she wasn't supposed to, no doubt about it.

And sure enough, having not spotted Hannah directly behind her at the back of the room, Brooklyn took the opportunity to lash out with her foot, square into the leg of Dayton sitting in the next row over. She was lightning fast, and if Hannah hadn't been looking straight at them when it happened, she never would've seen it.

"Oooowwwwwwwww!" Dayton howled, doubling over and clutching at his leg. "What'd you do that for?" he demanded, staring up at Brooklyn.

The classroom broke out in an excited babble, all concentration on their work completely gone. Meanwhile, Brooklyn was batting her eyes innocently at Dayton and was just opening up her mouth to claim ignorance when Hannah was on her, pulling her out of her chair and towards the door before Brooklyn could add lying to her list of crimes.

"Amelia, I'll be right back," she called over her shoulder. "Students, get back to work." And then she shut the door to the classroom behind her and stared down at Brooklyn, her arms folded across her chest. Brooklyn stared defiantly back up at her, her gray-green eyes an exact copy of her father's. She was a miniature, female version of Elijah Morland.

A little creepy, that.

"Okay, Brooklyn, why'd you do it?" Hannah asked, her tone strict. She might be a wallflower in a room full of adults, but she was large and in charge with her students.

But Brooklyn didn't break. She just stared back up at her defiantly, not saying a word.

"Brooklyn, I saw you do it," Hannah said, exasperated. "I'd just finished hanging up a picture on the wall when you looked around for me, didn't see me at the back of the room, and so you leaned right over and kicked Dayton, clear as day."

Brooklyn's eyes widened at that; it was a look of respect for the fact that a teacher had figured out what she was up to. It never failed – every student thought that they were the first ones to come up with mischievous ideas.

And then it disappeared and she was back to glaring up at her teacher, her angry bravado shielding her.

Hannah swallowed her groan. This class had already been more of a struggle to get settled into a routine than past classes had been. She really didn't want to add an openly defiant troublemaker to the mix. Mr. Pettengill's warning about keeping her thumb on Brooklyn from the very beginning flashed through her mind, but she pushed the thought away. Whatever the answer was with Brooklyn, treating her like a hardened criminal wasn't it.

"C'mon, let's go back inside the classroom," Hannah said, her frustration bleeding through her self control and right into her voice. "Move your stuff to the desk in the back. I think some time away from everyone else is a good idea."

Brooklyn shrugged nonchalantly, her dirty blonde hair swinging as she turned back towards the classroom door.

As Hannah followed Brooklyn back into the classroom, she realized just how dirty Brooklyn's dirty blonde hair really was. It wasn't just a darker blonde color, it was quite literally *dirty*. Her scalp looked like she hadn't washed it for a week.

Automatically, her eyes scanned down the back of Brooklyn, noticing how short and tight her jeans were, like they were her jeans from last school year. Had Brooklyn been wearing new school clothes previous to today? Most students were still wearing their new back-to-school clothes, not yet covered in grime or ripped to pieces and definitely not too small for them. That was something that would change soon enough, of course, but not usually by this point in the school year.

Brooklyn morosely picked up her stuff from her desk and moved to the back, shooting a dark look at Dayton as she walked past him. Something was going on between those two, and Hannah was going to figure out what it was. Dayton didn't tend to hang out with or interact with girls all that much – Hannah wasn't sure if he'd so much as said hello to a girl since the beginning of school, preferring to hang out with his buddies instead.

So when did Brooklyn have the chance to get that angry with him?

Hoping for some answers, Hannah pulled him out into the hallway to chat with him, but at least according to him, he had no idea what had caused Brooklyn to lash out.

Some days, the drama between ten year olds was just too much to bear.

While Amelia took the class to first recess, Hannah tried calling Brooklyn's mother, Sarah, but got no answer. Frustrated, she waited to call again after school, and this time, she hit pay dirt.

"Yeah?" Sarah answered the phone, the word sounding slightly…slurred?

That couldn't be right. Hannah glanced over at the clock on the wall. It was 3:22 in the afternoon. Sarah wasn't actually drunk.

Right?

"Hi, Ms. Morland," she said formally, gripping the phone with all of her might, "this is Hannah Lambert from the school. We had a bit of an incident today in class. Brooklyn…well, she kicked another student this morning pretty hard. She refuses to tell me why or what caused it. I—"

"Whysa hell is dat your business?" the woman snarl-slurred.

Now that Hannah had heard her speak an entire sentence, she was sure of it – Sarah Morland was completely snookered at three o'clock in the afternoon.

*Dear God above, save me.*

"It's my business because it's my classro—"

And that's when the phone line went dead.

The woman had hung up on Hannah. She'd actually hung up on her.

Hannah buried her head in her hands with a groan, listlessly letting the phone drop back into the cradle. Mr. Pettengill had said that Brooklyn was going to be a lot of trouble.

Hannah was starting to think that he'd named off the wrong Morland.

She slowly opened her eyes and looked wearily at the piles of papers stacked on every conceivable spot across her worn wooden desk, waiting to be graded or sorted or put away or thrown away or...

She stood up and grabbed her purse, forcing herself not to stuff a sheaf of papers into it to take home. She was going to go home and after a nice long ride on Wildflower, she was going to pull out one of her coloring books and relax a little. Do nothing more strenuous than decide which color to use next. She normally visited Dad every other Tuesday, but...she just didn't have it in her tonight. She could take one week off, right?

After today, she darn well deserved it.

# CHAPTER 5

ELIJAH

THE LUNCH BELL RANG, and like magic, every classroom door opened and kids came spilling out into the hallway, all heading towards the downstairs cafeteria in a stream of excited noise. Elijah leaned the handle of his mop against the painted dull gray cinder block of the hallway, humming to himself, excited to see Brooksy and hear about her day so far. He didn't actually need to be in this hallway right now, but hell, that was one of the few good things about being a janitor – he was in charge of the whole school, and as long as he got his work done, he was a-okay to take his lunch break when and where he wanted.

And when and where he wanted to, was with his daughter.

Brooksy looked both ways in the crowded hallway, trying to spot him, and when she did, her face lit up and she hurried his way, her blonde hair swinging with every step. She was his mini-me, and he loved her all the more because of it.

When he was a kid, he had blond hair that got darker by the year, until it ended up a dark brown without any blond at all. He'd told Brooksy this a year or so ago, and ever since, she'd wondered out loud more than once when was it that her hair was gonna "go brown like Daddy's."

No, it wasn't hard to love Brooksy at all.

"Hi, Dad!" she exclaimed, slipping her tiny hand into his calloused one. "Where we gonna eat today?"

"I didn't pack a lunch, so I thought we could eat on down in the cafeteria—"

"Mr. Morland!"

His head jerked up, and he saw Hannah bearing down on him, her blue eyes flashing behind her thick coke-bottle glasses. "I need to meet with you after school," she informed him crisply. "Are you available?"

Elijah was just sure his jaw was scraping the floor. He had the vaguest of memories of Hannah Lambert in high school – she'd been a senior when he was a freshman, so they hadn't exactly been the best of friends. All he could remember 'bout her back then was that she was as quiet as a mouse; as flashy and memorable as a wall painted white.

At the beginning of the school year, when he'd checked in with each teacher in their classrooms, she hadn't appeared to have changed one bit. The times that he'd cleaned her classroom since then and she'd been working away at her desk, she hadn't said more than two words to him.

Total.

But now…

Instinctively, Elijah looked down at his daughter, who looked as guilty as hell and was trying to hide behind his leg. She was ten. She was way too old to fit behind his leg, and she damn well knew it.

But she was clinging to it with all of her might anyway.

He looked back up at Hannah, who was still waiting for a reply, and who still looked way more…confrontational than he'd known she could be.

*Shit on a stick, what did Brooksy do?*

"I'll come on by your classroom after school is out," he promised, and then began shuffling off the best he could down the hallway, his daughter apparently now attached to him permanently. Most of the children had disappeared, leaving the hallways quieter than they'd been just minutes before. There were a few bangs and shouts from lingering children, but they were otherwise alone.

"Wanna tell me what's going on?" he asked the barnacle on his leg. She shook her head. She still wasn't making eye contact. "I can't talk to Miss Lambert 'bout you real well if you don't tell me what's going on." She shook her head. They were nearing the top of the staircase, about to go on down to the cafeteria. "I can't walk down these stairs if you don't let go of my leg." She hesitated for a moment at that, and then heaving a sigh, finally let go. He looked down at the top of her head. "You can talk to me, Brooksy," he said softly. "Just tell me what's going on."

Jerkily, she shook her head and then raced down the stairs ahead of him, disappearing through the doors of the cafeteria before he was even halfway down.

Yup, she was his mini-me all right. When he was in trouble, or even thought he was gonna get in trouble, he shut down. Brick walls talked more than he did when he saw problems brewing on the horizon.

With a sigh of his own, he headed into the cafeteria after his daughter. The meeting with Hannah after school was gonna be about as much fun as a tar-and-featherin' would be, and with his daughter refusing to say a word, he was going into it with his hands tied behind his back.

For the thousandth time, he wondered how it was that he could be a father and yet be so stupid. As a kid, he'd thought his parents knew everything. Now, he realized that they just made shit up as they went along, hoping for the best. He'd butted heads with his father more times than he could count growing up, and they didn't see eye to eye on most anything even now, but he was starting to empathize with the man anyway.

Which was a hell of a thing to realize.

# CHAPTER 6

## HANNAH

S HE HEARD A LIGHT RAP on the door frame and even before she could look up to see who it was, she knew it was Mr. Morland. The sparks of electricity shooting through her…

Yeah, it was him.

But still, when she looked up and saw his dark-haired form coming towards her, she swallowed. Hard. Where did this attraction come from? She hadn't felt this way in high school. She hadn't felt this way the times she'd seen him around town since then.

Did it really have to appear right now? This year? Right when she was supposed to be his daughter's teacher?

She stood up and skirted her desk so she could shake his hand in greeting. She honestly would've rather swallowed live snakes than leave the safety and comfort of her desk behind, but good manners dictated that she did so, and she always had good manners.

His stormy gray-green eyes glared down at her as they shook hands, and even before she could open her mouth to thank him for coming, he practically snarled, "So, what is it? I don't have all day."

She jerked her head and her hand back, and stared up at him as she crossed her arms in front of herself, rubbing the chills away that his touch had sent racing up her arms. She didn't want to feel chills up her arms around Mr. Morland, but she *especially* didn't if he was going to be a douchebag.

She bit back the retort dancing on the end of her tongue – *what, you have a lot of trash cans you need to hurry up and empty?* – and instead said evenly, "I wanted to talk to you because Brooklyn kicked a classmate yesterday as hard as she possibly could."

At which point, what happened was what always happened – the parent jumped to the child's defense. She could practically feel the arguments boiling up inside of him: He must've kicked her first. Or maybe Mr. Morland would start with the theory that the classmate must've deserved it. Oh, and then there was always the tried-and-true – Brooklyn didn't actually kick anyone and Hannah was mistaken.

Yada, yada, yada.

As a veteran teacher, Hannah had heard it all. She hurried on before Mr. Morland could spout off any of his misguided, this-is-my-baby-girl-and-I-must-stand-up-for-her-at-all-cost theories that would paint Brooklyn as the innocent victim.

"I was watching from the back of the classroom." She pointed to where she'd been standing, right in front of the terrarium. "Brooklyn sits there," she pointed at a desk only three rows from the back of the room, "and I watched as she looked around, trying to see where I was, but because I was directly behind her, she didn't spot me. So she kicked out her foot as hard as she could, right into the shin of Dayton who sits in that desk in the next aisle over." Hannah focused on only delivering the facts; facts that even the most ardent and loving parent couldn't refute. "The classroom had been quiet; the students had all been on task and working hard. I've never so much as seen Dayton and Brooklyn talk to each other before this. He's your typical boy – girls are icky and have germs, so he doesn't interact with them unless forced to. He wasn't even looking at her when it happened. But she refuses to tell me what's going on."

Her plan failed.

She could feel it rolling off him in waves – he didn't believe her. Or maybe he did believe her but he was going to argue anyway.

Hannah felt anger and frustration rise up in her chest. Why oh why were parents always like this? Why did they never want to believe that their child could be anything less than a perfect angel at school, even though they caused plenty of problems at home? Somehow, some way, parents believed that their kids had personality transplants every day when they came to school, and then their angel-like perfection disappeared each time on the way home.

Yup, it was written all over his face – he didn't believe a word she'd just told him.

"So," she demanded angrily, truly and thoroughly pissed off now, "is this typical for your daughter? Does she always go around kicking kids who haven't done a thing to her?"

Her libido could go jump in a lake. Never had it been so very wrong about the male specimen.

"Well now," he growled back, his eyebrows drawing together as he glowered down at her, "just 'cause you didn't see anything doesn't mean that it didn't happen before school or during recess or—"

"Mr. Morland," Hannah interrupted him crisply, "this is my twelfth year teaching. I am well aware that students can get into fights or arguments out of the range of my eyes and ears. The problem is, Brooklyn refuses to tell me what's going on. I talked to Dayton and he claims ignorance. Sure, kids say things all the time to get out of trouble, but in the fifth grade, they're not good at lying yet, thank God, and I can assure you, Dayton really has no clue. So, I've come to you – are there problems with

Brooklyn this school year? What has she been telling you at home?"

"We don't see each other outside of school!" he retorted, pissed at her and not even trying to hide it. "So your guess is as good as mine!"

"You don't see each other…?" Hannah repeated softly, totally confused. She knew that Sarah had primary custody of Brooklyn, but to not see each other at all…

And then it made sense. The missing pieces of the puzzle fitted into place.

*Duh.*

No wonder he'd left Mr. Petrol's and had gotten a job as the Cleveland Elementary School janitor. Being the night manager for Mr. Petrol's was probably not his dream job, but she couldn't imagine that being a school janitor was any better and most likely worse. For weeks now, she'd been trying to figure out what had made him decide that what he really wanted to do with his life was clean up puke and scrape bubble gum off every conceivable surface.

Now that she understood…it explained so much.

She felt a rush of understanding and admiration run through her at the dedication of the man in front of her. Not willing to let his ex-wife win what appeared to be an epic custody battle, he'd taken up mopping and garbage dumping just so he could see his daughter during the school day.

Now *that* was impressive.

# CHAPTER 7

## ELIJAH

D*AMMIT!* He hadn't meant to let that slip. Admitting to people that he couldn't even see his own daughter whenever he wanted to; that his ex-wife had that much control over his life…

It sucked ass.

And what sucked even more was the pity he saw in Hannah's eyes. He didn't want pity from her. He didn't want pity from anyone.

"Is Sarah fighting you in court over custody?" she asked quietly, her blue eyes distorted behind the thick lenses of her glasses.

He had a fleeting moment where he wondered what she'd look like without those damned glasses on, and then he shoved that thought away. *Don't go there, Eli.*

"Yeah," he admitted begrudgingly. "After her parents died in that car wreck outside of town, she's been using all of her inheritance to beat me in court. Sad to say, money usually wins."

Yeah, he was bitter. He wasn't afraid to admit it.

"So that's why you became the janitor here," Hannah said

slowly, as if stating a simple fact out loud that solved a long-standing mystery.

"Well...I...how did you know?" he sputtered indignantly. Why he took this job was a personal thing, and not something he discussed openly. As in, with anyone at all. His brother Aaron had guessed at the reason when Elijah had told him about the job change, but Elijah had refused to dignify that guess with a response. He didn't like other people in his business.

And he sure as hell didn't like that Hannah had figured it out.

"You can't see Brooklyn after school or on the weekends because her mother is fighting you – and winning – in court, so you took a job here so you could see her during lunch and recess. Not exactly a Sherlock-Holmes moment for me, Mr. Morland," she said dryly.

"No one else has figured it out," he protested.

"Or they did and they just haven't said anything to you," she countered.

*Huh.*

Truth be told, that was an even more awful idea. People standing around and jawing about him? Just the idea of it sent chills racing down his spine.

Desperate to talk about something else – anything else – he realized that his best chance at a quick getaway was to tell the woman what she wanted to hear and get his ass out of her classroom ASAP.

"I'll talk to Brooksy tomorrow," he promised begrudgingly. "See if I can get anything outta her."

Already, he was dreading the conversation. Considering how closed-mouth Brooksy was being about the whole thing, chances were that he was more likely to get water from a rock, but hell, he'd give it the ol' college try. Maybe he'd pack a lunch and they could sit together in his janitor's closet and chat. Without anywhere to escape to, she'd have to talk.

Or, they could have the world's quietest lunch. Really, it was 50/50 at this point.

Tugging on the brim of his baseball cap, he hurried outta Hannah's room before she could give him any more pity-filled stares from behind those damn ugly glasses.

# CHAPTER 8

## HANNAH

ANNAH TOOK A SIP of her delicious black coffee as she listened to her besties whine that Gage Dyer didn't seem to realize that any of them existed.

Or, more to the point, drool over his muscles while whining that he didn't know they existed.

*Who says you can't multitask?*

"He can pick me up and swing me over his shoulder anytime he wants to," Carla sighed dreamily, her chin propped in her hand as she watched Gage, the owner, baker, and current delivery boy of the Muffin Man, carry a 50-pound sack of flour on his shoulder into the back of the bakery. Carla was the owner of Happy Petals, the only flower shop in town, and she had to be the most romantic, starry-eyed person Hannah had ever met. There wasn't a person on the planet better suited to be a flower shop owner than Carla. She believed, with all of her heart and soul, that true love was out there for every person who just wanted it enough.

Which just made it all the more depressing that she was the Vice President of the Early Spinster's Club.

"He's one of the few men in town who *could* throw me over

his shoulder and carry me around," Michelle said admiringly as the two of them openly watched Gage go back for another sack of flour. Michelle ran the city's animal shelter and as much as Carla loved flowers and romance, that's how much Michelle loved animals. In fact, Hannah was a little surprised that Michelle was even drooling over Gage. As far as Hannah knew, Gage didn't own a single animal, which she sort of assumed took him right off the eligibility list in Michelle's eyes.

"Those muscles," Michelle whispered. "I bet he could wrestle a Great Dane into compliance without even breaking into a sweat."

*Ah.*

And there it was – the reason why Michelle was willing to overlook Gage's lack of ownership of an animal.

Well, and as President of the Early Spinster's Club, maybe Michelle was becoming less finicky about potential dates as time went on. Sawyer, Idaho wasn't exactly bristling with handsome, single men interested in the three of them. Their best shot, Adam Whitaker – the local vet and a hunky man in his own right – had hooked up with Kylie VanLueven over the summer. Adam was a real sweetie, but despite Hannah's best efforts, he'd never so much as looked at her twice.

Which, to be clear, her "best effort" was her asking him to come to her classroom and give presentations on being a vet to her fifth-grade students. For her, that was practically like her stripping down and throwing herself across his lap while yelling, "Take me, take me, your willing sex slave!"

Practically just like that.

He'd always been willing to come and present, of course – he was one of the most genuinely nice people she'd ever met – but that was as far as it got. For her, anyway. Kylie VanLueven had been a student of hers many moons ago, so the fact that Adam had started dating her instead…

It sure didn't help Hannah feel like less of an old maid, that was for darn sure.

Hannah watched with a detached, clinical interest as Gage walked by again, yet another sack of flour flung carelessly over his shoulder like he was carrying a bag of feathers, muscles bulging and rippling with every step. She sighed as she wrinkled her nose. He was cute, yeah – even a blind person could see that – but he was just so…so muscular. He looked like he'd smoosh her flat in bed. She didn't need or even desire a guy with muscles bulging everywhere. She liked them a little more sleek.

Strong, sure, but not in-your-face strong.

Capable of getting things done, but not of bench-pressing a caboose after breakfast.

Oh, and absolutely, definitely, 100% should not be the father of a student.

Was that too much to ask?

She heaved another sigh.

"…Earth to Hannah!" Michelle practically hollered, snapping her fingers in front of Hannah's nose. Startled, Hannah whipped her head back and stared at her friend in surprise.

"You've been in your own little world for ages," Carla put in kindly, as always trying to play the part of the peacemaker and smoother-outer-of-waters. "What're you thinking about?"

"And what was that sigh all about?" Michelle asked bluntly.

"Sigh? I sighed?" Hannah asked, taken aback. She tried to remember what'd just happened.

Had she sighed? And if she had, surely it wasn't that big of a deal, right?

"Like the weight of the world is on your shoulders," Michelle supplied.

"Orrrr…" Carla said brightly, ever the optimist, "you were thinking about someone. So, tell us, who was it?" she asked eagerly, assuming – as always – that love was at the bottom of every sigh and tear and smile.

"I was just thinking—" Hannah waved her hand in the air dismissively. "You know. Things."

Michelle and Carla cocked their eyebrows at her in a matching move that Hannah wasn't sure if it should make her laugh or cry.

"Well, that muscles are…they can be too much of a good thing. You know? I like 'em more…compact. Less likely to crush me on accident or something." She waved her hand around again. "Like Elijah Morland," she added. Just for demonstrative purposes, of course. Not that she'd been thinking of him in particular, but just as an example. "Slender, well built, plenty of muscles, but not *too* many."

Michelle and Carla stared at her like she'd just sprouted a horn out of her forehead.

"What?" she finally asked defensively.

"Holy cow," Michelle said, whistling her amazement, "Hannah Lambert has gone and fallen in love."

And then they were busy snatching her glasses off her face and talking about contacts and maybe she should get her hair layered but being such a beautiful red color, she didn't need to dye it. Someone – Hannah thought it was Carla but it was hard to tell since the world had just become this wavy, indistinct place filled with moving dark blobs – was running their fingers through her hair and holding it up as they talked about what could be done to it and quoting lines about "true love" from *Princess Bride*, which meant that it was totally Carla manhandling her hair since that was the movie she was obsessed with, and—

"Stop!" Hannah bellowed.

The two fell silent along with the rest of the Muffin Man, not a sound to be heard in the bakery as Hannah glared at her two best friends.

They were, no doubt, shocked to their core that Hannah had actually yelled something. Well, she could only guess that's what was happening since she couldn't see their faces, but she was pretty sure they were probably shocked.

They'd joked, more than once, that Hannah wouldn't yell if her hair was on fire.

Darn it all, maybe she'd yell if they were talking about *layering* her hair. They just hadn't realized it until today.

She squinted as hard as she could, until she spotted something that looked vaguely like her glasses, and snatched them out of someone's hands. Shoving them back onto her face, she glowered at the two women she'd previously loved with all of her might. That love was starting to disappear the longer they talked about cutting her hair like she was some mannequin without an opinion of her own.

"I'm not in love," she hissed as the bakery finally resumed its normal noisy chatter around them. "I was just…using an example. I've been seeing him a lot lately at the school, so he just happened to be the guy who popped into my head."

They continued to stare at her, not saying a word, their facial expressions saying it all for them.

"And even if I was," she finally protested when the silence became too much to bear, "it wouldn't matter. He's the father of one of my students, he's my coworker, and oh, then there's my dad…can you even imagine? What a disaster *that* would be. Then there's my kids this year…I'm having a way harder time with bullying and fighting than I ever have before. The class just isn't coming together as a cohesive whole and I don't know what to do about it. I've got cute little girls kicking boys and parents drunk as a skunk at 3:30 in the afternoon and…and I can't. I just can't."

She crossed her arms defensively and glared self-righteously at the two of them. There. She'd told them.

Michelle and Carla just sat there for a moment longer, and then Carla said softly, "Are you sure about that? Or do you just not want to take a chance on love?"

Hannah settled back against the slick leather of the booth, staring down at her now-cold coffee.

She hated the question.

Hated that Carla thought to ask it.

Hated that Carla might be right.

# CHAPTER 9

## ELIJAH

"ALL RIGHT, Brooksy, truth time," Elijah said bluntly. His daughter's feet were hanging off the edge of the five-gallon bucket, not quite reaching the ground as they sat and ate lunch in his closet. The smell of cleaning supplies was overpowering but as Elijah figured, it was just part of putting the screws into his daughter. Maybe she'd be more likely to talk to him if she wasn't happy about being cooped up in there with him.

"I talked to Miss Lambert yesterday," he continued, "and she told me about you kicking Dayton. She says he doesn't know what the hell is going on – why you're mad at him – and that you aren't talking either."

Silence.

"Brooksy, you gotta talk to me. Is Dayton beating you up after school? Is he teasing you while you're standing in line? Is he pulling your hair? You gotta tell me what's going on."

"He ain't bein' mean to me," Brooksy burst out and then clamped her mouth shut so tight, he wondered if he'd have to use a crowbar to get it open again.

"He isn't being mean to *you*?" Eli repeated slowly. "But, is he being mean to someone else?"

Silence.

"Brooksy—" he said warningly, his patience just about gone.

"Juan Miller," she burst out. "Dayton called him a spic. Dad, what's a spic?"

Eli was choking and gasping for air as he stared at his ten-year-old daughter. How was it her classmates were using language like that? She was too little for that shit.

And then, it hit him. "Hold on, how come you're upset about Dayton calling Juan that, if you don't know what it means?"

She rolled her eyes, a ten year old going on seventeen. "The way he said it," she told him in her best 'duh' voice. "It wasn't a compliment, that's for sure."

"No, it wasn't that," Elijah said dryly.

"So, what does it mean?" Brooksy persisted.

Elijah rubbed at his jaw, his sandwich forgotten in his other hand as he stared down at his daughter. His mini-me.

He didn't want to have this conversation with her; he really, really didn't.

But she was just like her momma in some ways – when she wanted to, she could make stainless steel seem downright pliable, and she'd keep going after this like a dog after a bone until she got her answer. It was best that he be the one to give it to her.

"Juan…he's Abby and Wyatt's little boy, right?" Elijah said, stalling for time.

"Kinda," Brooksy replied, her forehead squished up as she tried to sort it out in her head. "He says it's gonna be official at the end of October. What does that mean?"

Here, finally, was a topic that Elijah were more comfortable talking about. The Millers were quite a bit older than him, by about five or six years, but still, everyone in town knew their story and what they'd gone through together, and about Juan's past. If Eli was a romantic – which he damn well wasn't – even he'd be inclined to say that they were a match made in heaven, because after all, who else other than Abby would be willing to put up with a stubborn son-of-a-bitch like Wyatt?

"Abby and Wyatt Miller are adopting him – making him their own," he told Brooksy. "Like you're my daughter – Juan is gonna be their son, forever." He paused for a moment, searching for just the right words for the next part. "His…uh… his biological parents aren't, you know, real good people, you see, so they gave him up—"

"His parents sold little girls to other people," Brooksy interrupted him, sounding official, as if she knew exactly what that meant.

Elijah felt ill again. His daughter was learning the word "spic" and all about human trafficking? He was suddenly wishing very hard that he was back to changing her diapers. He'd hated to do it back then, of course, but now…

He'd take a real doozy of a diaper over this any day of the week.

"And they weren't nice to him, either," she added. "He likes his parents now. They feed him every day – good food, even – and they don't leave him places with strangers for weeks and weeks."

"That's…that's good," Elijah finally managed, not sure what else to say. It *was* good, of course, but that wasn't a hell of a high bar to leap over, and the fact that Juan had ever had parents that did otherwise made Eli wanna rearrange some noses.

"So, what's a spic?" Brooksy persisted.

*Dammit.* Her long attention span sure as hell didn't come from him. When he was her age, he could hardly sit still for more than two minutes at a time, always wanting to be off running and playing and jumping, not exactly a trait that his teachers had appreciated.

Brooksy, on the other hand, could sit and focus on something for what seemed like hours. *Especially* if that "something" wasn't something he wanted to discuss.

He looked at her and found that her gray-green eyes – an exact match to his – were still pinned on him. He sighed.

"That's a…not nice way of saying he's Hispanic," Elijah finally settled on. "He's from Mexico, right? Well, this is a mean way of saying that."

"Is it bad to be from Mexico?"

The urge to run and move and be anywhere but there at that moment was just as strong as it'd been when he'd been in fifth grade. He shifted on his bucket-cum-seat.

"No, not at all," he reassured her. "Mexico is just another country, like the US is a country. Some people are just assholes."

"That's Dayton all right," Brooksy said morosely. "He's a great, big asshole."

"Brooksy!" Elijah choked out.

"What?" she volleyed back defensively. "You're the one who said it."

Elijah squeezed his eyes shut. When he'd found out Sarah was pregnant, he hadn't been happy, of course, and had spent nine months dreading the idea of changing a baby's diaper and trying to get 'em to go to sleep and living through screaming fits…

But as soon as they laid the reddest, most wrinkled, ugliest baby in the world in his arms, he'd fallen in love with her on the spot. He was gonna be a perfect daddy. He was never gonna screw anything up. He was never gonna swear around her or get angry and yell or anything.

Ten years later…

Well, that hadn't exactly worked out the way he'd been planning.

"Why didn't you tell Miss Lambert about this?" Elijah asked, deciding to sidestep the swearing issue for the moment. He'd figure out what to do on that topic later. "If Dayton was calling Juan bad names, why didn't you tell Miss Lambert?"

"I thought Juan would get in trouble," Brooksy said,

shrugging. "I didn't know what 'spic' meant, but I knew it wasn't nice, so maybe Juan would be in trouble for being it."

Elijah tried to follow the convoluted ten-year-old logic but got lost about halfway through.

"Dayton keeps telling Juan that they have to meet up by the swing set after school," she continued matter-of-factly. "Dayton wants to fight. Juan can't do it; Abby or Wyatt is always there right after school to pick him up. Dayton says that he's a scaredy cat and that's why he won't fight. But Juan isn't. Juan is the nicest boy in the whole fifth grade!" she finished loyally.

Elijah opened up his mouth to point out that being the nicest boy in the whole fifth grade didn't mean that he wasn't also a scaredy cat, but then decided against it. He wasn't about to egg on a fight between a racist bully and an adopted kid who'd been through enough trauma to last a lifetime.

"You have to tell Miss Lambert what's going on," Elijah said instead. "Your teacher…she'll listen. Juan won't be in trouble, I promise."

Brooksy looked at him skeptically, clearly unconvinced.

"She's one of the good ones," he promised her. He wasn't sure what caused him to say that – he hardly knew Hannah at all. She was too damn quiet to know a thing about her. But somehow, it felt…right. He knew the words were true, even if he couldn't say why. "But Brooks, you can't just go around kicking bullies in the leg."

Even as the words came out of his mouth, he hated himself for it. When he'd been a kid and he'd been told to go talk to an adult whenever something bad had happened, all he could think was that his parents and his teachers didn't have a damn clue of what it was really like out on the playground. If they had, they never would've given him such dumbass advice.

Now that he was an adult and a parent…he could see it. It sure wasn't fun and he sure didn't like it, but dammit all, they'd been right. He couldn't just go around, avenging the wrongs of the world whenever he wanted.

No, that was Aaron's job.

Why didn't Elijah become a cop like his brother? There were more than a few people he'd like to kick in the shins if given half a chance.

He forced himself to focus, and began ticking the items off on his fingers. "You need to talk to Miss Lambert about Dayton and Juan; you can't kick Dayton in the shins anymore; and you shouldn't *ever* use the word that Dayton used."

"Don't say 'spic'?" Brooksy asked, her forehead wrinkled with confusion.

"Yeah, that word," Elijah said dryly. "It's not a nice one. It's much worse than 'asshole.'"

"Does that mean I can say 'ass—'"

"Brooksy!" Elijah cut her off, glaring at her. The laughing grin died away as she looked up at him and saw that he wasn't kidding.

"Sorry, Dad," she mumbled.

Yeah, he'd take a stinky diaper over a swearing ten-year-old any day of the week.

# CHAPTER 10

## HANNAH

As Hannah reached for the next pile of papers to grade, the fluorescent light bulb overhead began flickering. Again. Almost immediately, the strobe lighting started wreaking its usual effect: An awful headache.

"I really hate you," she mumbled up at the light fixture as she walked over to the doorway of the classroom to flick the switch off. She'd choose to sit through three – no, make that four – professional development classes rather than submit a work order to the school district to get repairs done, but at this point, she really didn't have a choice.

It wouldn't be so bad except the head of maintenance, Mr. Fuhlman, made it his personal goal in life to—

"I can help you with that," a male voice said right in her ear.

She screamed and yelped and spun in a half-circle with her hand clasped over her mouth, her heart going a million miles an hour, to find Mr. Morland looking down at her and laughing.

"I'm sorry," he said, holding up a hand placatingly, looking not a bit sorry at all. "I didn't mean to scare you. I just thought I'd offer to help ya out." He squinted up at the turned-off light fixture. "Flickering a bunch on you?"

"Yes. It's enough to—"

She stopped. He didn't want to hear about how it gave her headaches. People didn't care about that sort of thing about her. She just wasn't interesting enough.

He waited for a moment for her to continue, but when she didn't, he flipped the switch on the wall again, bringing the flickering fixture to life.

"Hmmm…" he said, studying the godawful light for a moment before thankfully flipping it back off again. "I'll take care of it for you," he promised, turning back to her. "That way, you don't have to talk to Mr. Fuhlman about it. It isn't nice to talk bad of others, but…"

He trailed off.

Usually almost mute around the male species – at least around the ones taller than her – Hannah felt the bizarre compulsion to tell Mr. Morland a too-strange-to-be-true-and-yet-it-was story about Mr. Fuhlman.

Just because it seemed like he'd enjoy it.

"Last week," she blurted out before she could come to her senses, "he blamed Mrs. Crofts for the fact that a ceiling tile had fallen on a student while she was teaching. Said it was her fault for not doing regular maintenance on the ceiling and keeping it in good shape."

Mr. Morland bust up laughing, his eyes crinkling delightfully with contagious humor. Hannah watched him closely, trying to figure out if he was just humoring her or if he honest to Pete thought she was funny. "I missed that one," he admitted when he finally stopped laughing. "I'm not surprised, though. Is, uh, is the kid okay?"

*Either he's the world's best actor, or he really did think I was funny.*

She wasn't sure what to think about that. Something that insanely crazy didn't happen every day.

"Yeah, it mostly hit the desk," she responded, forcing herself to talk rather than just hurry and hide behind her desk again like every nerve-ending in her body was telling her to do.

"Surprised the heck out of everyone, of course, but the student's fine." Right in the middle of this spate of words that she wasn't even quite sure where they were coming from, an attack of guilt overwhelmed her, making her feel bad for bad-mouthing the older gentleman. "Mr. Fuhlman – he's good at fixing things, he is," she hurried on. "He just…he gives out a lot of guff before he gets to the fixing part of things."

"That's an awful nice way of saying it," Mr. Morland said dryly. "Your problem is easy enough to fix, though. It's just your ballast – it's going out. I'll need to get supplies to replace it, so it won't be until tomorrow after school that I can work on it. Is that soon enough?"

"Sure," she said, grateful and a little awed that he was still talking to her. She casually clasped her hands behind her back and pinched her arm as hard as she could.

*Ouch!*

Yup, she was definitely awake.

She gingerly rubbed at the sore spot as she asked, "How do you know about ballasts? Did this happen a lot at Mr. Petrol's?"

He shrugged nonchalantly. "Nah, we had a contract for all of our maintenance there. I never did more than plunge a toilet when I had to. But I had this same problem with the light in my garage. Did a YouTube search to figure out how to fix it. Pretty straightforward."

"Not to me, it isn't," she mumbled. She had all of the mechanical skills of a drunk monkey high on cocaine. Asking her to fix something…she had a better chance of figuring out how to fly to the moon the following Thursday.

"Brooksy talked to you about Dayton, right?" Mr. Morland asked, interrupting her self-deprecating thoughts. "About his language and such?"

"Yes," Hannah said, keeping a straight face like any proper elementary teacher should, but his question reminded her of the discussion she'd had with Brooklyn, and…well, she bust up laughing. Also not something she did often around men. "I meant to say – you must've given her quite the talking to about language. She kept going the rounds with me, refusing to say what Dayton had called Juan because you'd told her not to use that word anymore. I finally had to cross-my-heart-and-hope-to-die promise that I wouldn't be mad at her and reassure her that it was okay to repeat a word but not to say it in anger. Still, she whispered it in my ear."

*All*

*These*

*Words*

*Where are they coming from? Have aliens taken over my body?*

Mr. Morland looked at her and grinned, revealing a slight crossover of his two front teeth that she hadn't noticed before. It made his smile even more endearing than it would've been otherwise.

Which, considering how her heart was racing at the moment, Hannah didn't figure she really needed much help appreciating these finer points, and yet…

"I, uhhh, might've made that point pretty clear," he admitted. "I just didn't want her running around, spouting it off to anyone who stood still for more than three seconds at a time."

"No, that wouldn't be good," Hannah agreed soberly. "I will be talking to Dayton's parents about that language; my worry is, that's who he learned it…" She trailed to a stop.

She really couldn't gossip about the parents of her students with other parents of her students. That broke like ten ethics rules.

Hannah was many things, but rule-breaker? Not on that list.

"Well anyway," she said in an overly bright voice, "I'm glad we figured it out." She still had a classroom full of fighting and bullying and she had no idea how to bring the class together as a cohesive whole, but at least one mystery was solved. "We talked about how she can't just kick Dayton whenever he isn't being nice to Juan; she informed me – pretty morosely – that you'd already told her that. She didn't seem happy about it."

"She's my mini-me," Mr. Morland said with a laugh. "Seeing wrongs in the world…she wants to fix 'em herself. After her karate chop to that kid's leg, I'm thinking she should look at becoming a cop or something."

*Mini-me*…listening to Mr. Morland talk about his daughter was ridiculously adorable. His willingness to become a janitor so he could see Brooklyn; his obvious love and pride in her…

Yeah, he was impressive as hell. As someone who'd lay down her life for her students and was all-too-often disappointed by parents who didn't seem to feel the same way about their own children, Mr. Morland was getting more attractive by the moment.

Which he really, really didn't need help with.

She gulped.

"I told her she could talk to you anytime," he said seriously, apparently completely oblivious to the thoughts racing through her mind. "She didn't seem to think that she could talk to a teacher 'bout what was happening, but I told her you were one of the good guys."

Hannah felt a large lump form in her throat from the kindness of his words. Did he have any idea how much they meant to her? She searched his face. He couldn't know.

He couldn't.

And then the story behind his words registered fully and Hannah gulped. "I…I understand her hesitation," she finally got out. "Her…uh…the teacher she had for fourth grade…he isn't…well, I guess I wouldn't choose him to teach a child of mine. If given the choice."

Which was going to go down in history as the largest understatement ever uttered. In her not-so-humble opinion, Mr. Pettengill shouldn't be in charge of teaching a pet rock, let alone a sentient being.

"She never talked much about Mr. Pettengill," he said after a moment, scratching at the stubble on his jaw as he thought. "I guess I didn't think to wonder why. I shoulda…So after a rough year with him, you think she isn't exactly fond of teachers anymore?"

"That's my guess. She doesn't trust me enough to tell me that, but…" She shrugged. "It makes sense."

He nodded slowly, and she could tell that something was bothering him, but he didn't say another word for a long time. So long, in fact, she began shifting from foot to foot, wondering how she could excuse herself from the conversation and go hide behind her desk when he finally spoke again.

"I'll be back tomorrow to work on the ballast," he said quietly, and then slipped out of the door, the clanking of the mop bucket starting up as he began pushing it down the hallway.

Hannah walked slowly back up to the front of the classroom and sank into her chair behind her desk, automatically adjusting her weight to accommodate for the wonkiness of the chair so she didn't pitch off it and onto the floor.

She was in trouble. Deep trouble.

Falling into lust with a student's father…

Deep, deep, *deep* trouble.

# CHAPTER 11

ELIJAH

H{E CLIMBED UP} the ladder and slid the cover off the broken light fixture. Below him, he could see Hannah hovering out of the corner of his eye, watching his every movement.

"You don't need to watch if you don't want to," he said as he carefully lowered the cover down to the floor and leaned it up against the ladder. "If you've got other things to do, you're free to go do 'em."

"Okay," she said agreeably, not moving an inch, her teeth worrying her bottom lip.

Elijah quit sneaking peeks at her out of the corner of his eye and got to work on the fixture. If she wanted to stand there and gawk at him while he worked, it wasn't any skin off his nose.

A couple of minutes passed by in absolute dead silence, other than the whine of his cordless drill and the occasional swear word he let loose when a screw got caught up in shit. And still, she didn't move. Prickles danced over his skin, making him antsy.

Did she really have to stand right there? Teachers were always claiming that they were busier than a one-legged man in a hopping contest, so how come she had all of this free time to stand around and just watch him work?

He opened up his mouth to give her a more pointed suggestion about how she ought to go do something else – anything else – when she blurted out, "Is Sarah having financial problems?"

He swung his head around so quickly, he wasn't watching what he was doing and he smashed it up against the dangling shroud. "Shit," he growled, rubbing at his head. He glared down at Hannah. "Sarah *isn't* my wife – we got a divorce over a year ago."

"I know that," she retorted. She was still worrying her bottom lip. He had to force himself to look away from her full lips and back towards her eyes, distorted behind the thick lenses. There, that was a better sight to focus on. "It's just that Brooklyn's clothes are ill-fitting, and I thought perhaps Sarah couldn't afford to buy her clothes this school year. Because of financial problems," she added.

Money and Sarah…those two topics combined together were guaran-damn-teed to piss him off, and sure enough, he felt the anger boil up slowly inside of him like a sleeping volcano coming to life.

"Oh, she's got money aplenty," he growled, turning back to the fixture and getting to work. "She got the max child support allowed under Idaho state law, which she doesn't need since her parents up and died, leaving her a fortune." He bit down on his tongue, feeling guilty for saying it. Her parents had never cared much for him but he hadn't wanted them dead. He certainly didn't wish roads covered with black ice on them.

He'd feel a whole lot worse about them dying if Sarah hadn't taken their life insurance payout as the excuse she'd been waiting for for years so she could divorce him.

She went for the max amount of child support possible not because she needed it, but because she knew it'd make Elijah's life miserable.

And boy howdy, had she succeeded.

"I don't know what the arrangements are between you and Sarah," Hannah said primly, "but I can say that Brooklyn's clothing appears to be from last school year, and much too small for her at this point."

"How do you know?" he growled, refusing to look down at her as he continued to work on the light. "Did you ask her?"

"No, I didn't need to. Her pants said it all."

He stopped and stared down at her. Hannah stared back up at him.

"They split today. Afternoon recess. She sat down in the swings and they just ripped apart."

He gulped, horrified. "Why didn't she tell me?" he whispered to himself. He'd seen her after school. She'd been chattering away about some art project they were working on in class. She didn't say anything 'bout her pants tearing apart.

Hannah shrugged. "She was probably embarrassed. The recess aide took her down to the principal's office and had her change there."

"Change? Into what?"

"A spare set of pants. We keep a big box of clothing down at the office for kids in case they ruin theirs by puking on them, bleeding all over them, or splitting them wide open on the swing set." She laughed a little, and Elijah grinned back. Just for a moment.

Then he turned back to the light fixture and got back to work. Dammit all, he needed to concentrate.

With his tongue tucked firmly between his teeth, he pulled the ground wire into place as he thought over what Hannah had just said. If she was telling the truth – and he couldn't figure why she'd lie about something like this – then the $200 that Sarah had claimed that she absolutely *had* to have to take Brooksy school shopping was spent on something else.

He'd been forced to pay his truck payment late 'cause of sending that money to Sarah, which had cost him a $50 fee. If she'd cost him that money just so she could go clothes shopping for herself…

He bit down hard on his tongue. He could strangle Sarah with his bare hands some days, he really could.

"Brooksy hasn't shown me any new clothes this year," he told Hannah as he continued to thread the wires through. He was too embarrassed to look the teacher in the eye as he spoke because he should've seen this for himself. He couldn't believe he let Sarah pull this one over on him. "Usually, Brooksy likes to show off all of her new clothes to me. This year, I gave her momma the money to take her shopping and then thought nothing more about it. I'll talk to Sarah this evening."

*And wring her scrawny little neck the next time I see her.*

"Thank you," Hannah said formally. "The school district can't say anything to her about sending Brooklyn to school in ill-fitting clothing; if she was to send Brooklyn to school in shorts and flip-flops in the middle of a blizzard, we could talk to her about that. But we can't critique a parent's clothing choices just because they're too small or large or out of date. That isn't our business."

Elijah nodded his understanding and then climbed down the ladder. "All done," he told her. Her eyes shot back up to the light fixture overhead.

"Really?!" she breathed. "So quickly?"

He leaned over and flipped the light switch, flooding the room with steady fluorescent lighting.

"That's amazing!" she exclaimed. She looked up at him, her gaze plainly saying that he not only hung the light fixture for her, he'd also hung the sun, the moon, and the stars for her.

He shifted on the balls of his feet uncomfortably. It felt nice – real nice – to be the guy who solved problems for a woman again.

Too nice.

"You're just brilliant with fixing things," she told him. "I could've watched a hundred YouTube videos and still not have been able to fix it. It's been giving me headaches for a good long while now; I can't believe it's fixed just like that."

He felt red creep up the base of his neck and he rubbed at it, trying to wish the tell-tale blush away. Other than Brooksy, he hadn't had a woman say nice things to him in a real long time, and anyway, Brooksy wasn't a woman.

He forced himself to make eye contact with Hannah, and then found himself wondering what her big blue eyes would look like without those thick lenses there to make 'em look like they were passing in front of a funny house mirror.

He would never know, of course, but he sure wanted to.

A lot.

# CHAPTER 12
## HANNAH

S HE WAS STANDING THERE, thinking he was a magician with a screwdriver one minute, and then he was leaning towards her the next. She froze in place, the absolutely insane idea running through her head that he was going to kiss her.

He couldn't / wouldn't / shouldn't kiss her, though.

Right?

And then his hands were pulling her glasses off and even as the world went wavy and indistinct, she heard him say, "I just…I wanted to know what you looked like. Without 'em on. I've been wondering ever since the start of school…"

He trailed off and was just staring at her, or at least she assumed he was staring at her – it was hard to tell, honestly – and she held her breath, her heart beating out of her chest. Maybe him kissing her wasn't such an insane idea after all. Maybe he was going to kiss her and maybe she'd let him and maybe she'd like it. Maybe—

He shoved the glasses back on her face, catawampus with the earpiece for her left ear sticking into her ear rather than going over it, and then he was hurrying away, his footsteps echoing in the empty hallway as he made a run for it.

Hannah pulled her glasses off and settled them back onto her face even as her heart slowed from its crazy rhythm to a painful one instead.

He'd wanted to know what she looked like without her glasses on, and the answer had sent him quite literally running away.

How had she been so delusional? Of *course* he wouldn't think she was beautiful. She'd been a senior when he was a freshman. She was the Secretary of the Early Spinster's Club.

No man thought she was beautiful, but especially not a man like Mr. Morland.

And she was okay with that, truly she was. She was happy with her life, just the way it was.

She wiped the tear off that was trailing down her face.

She couldn't be happier, honestly.

# CHAPTER 13

## ELIJAH

THE ECHOING SCREAMS of happy children rang in Elijah's ears, making his head hurt. He didn't mind listening to Brooksy scream and yell – well, there was that one note she liked to hit that made his eyes cross – but a whole passel of children…

There was a reason why he cleaned inside of the school while the kids were outside at recess.

The waitress slid their meat lover's pizza in front of them with an apology. "I don't know how the cook lost that part of the order," she said for what must've been the millionth time.

"It's fine – no problem at all," Aaron said sweetly, giving the harried waitress his best charming smile. She smiled back and leaned over to pick up a dirty napkin, letting her shirt gape away from her oversized chest as she went.

"We're good," Elijah told her curtly before she could really start to mooning over his older brother. He always was the charmer out of the two of them and could talk the socks right off a girl – quite literally – if he put his mind to it.

Picking up on the none-too-subtle briskness in Eli's voice, the waitress straightened up and told 'em to holler if they needed anything else before she hurried off, leaving the dirty napkin behind.

*Must not've been so important after all.*

Aaron shot him a disgruntled look.

"What?" Elijah asked innocently, scanning the ball pit for Brooksy and her friend, Juniper, to make sure they were still playing and having fun. Which, seriously, who names their child Juniper, for hell's sakes? When Elijah first met Juniper's mother, he'd made a joke about her daughter developing a gin drinking problem.

She didn't exactly start rolling around on the ground with laughter at the joke, that was for damn sure. It took a real long while before Juniper's mom had let Brooksy come over and play again.

After that, Eli kept his mouth shut when meeting other parents, especially the mothers. He didn't mind pissing 'em off – no skin off his nose – but it wasn't fair to Brooksy when she was punished for it.

He spotted them climbing up the ladder for the slide, screaming and laughing as they climbed like little monkeys over it all. Their cheese pizza had come ages ago and they'd already finished so they could go apeshit over the ball pit and slide and leave him and Aaron in peace for a moment.

"She seemed interested," Aaron grumped, bringing Eli's attention back to their conversation, or more specifically, his whining. "A couple more refills of my Coke, and I'd probably have her phone number."

Elijah rolled his eyes. Aaron was a collector of phone numbers and he left beautiful women in his wake everywhere he went. By this time next week, he'd probably have four more phone numbers to add to his list. He was only three years older than Elijah, but he was apparently trying to single-handedly make up for Eli's lack of experience with girls. Probably thought he was protecting the Morland name or something.

*Speaking of girls…*

Elijah took another peek at Brooksy and Juniper to make sure they were still laughing and screaming with delight, and then turned to Aaron. "Do you know Hannah Lambert?" he asked, just as his brother took a big bite of his meaty pizza.

Aaron chewed for a second, giving Elijah a chance to snag a piece of his own, and then said around a mouthful of cheese and ham chunks, "You mean that mousy chick over at the school? Wouldn't say 'boo' if you lit her hair on fire?"

"Yeah, that one," Elijah said slowly, although he didn't particularly care for how Aaron described her. There was a lot more to Hannah than that. When he got her to talk, why, she could be downright funny when she put her mind to it.

"What about her?" Aaron asked around another mouthful of pizza.

"I was just trying to decide if…well, I'm trying to figure out if I'm losing it or not. The other day, I'd swear she was the prettiest thing I'd ever laid eyes on."

Aaron gaped at him for a moment, and then started laughing. "Were you drunk?" he finally asked when he could breathe again.

"Of course not!" Elijah snapped, pissed at Aaron for his reaction. He didn't have to be such a dick all of the time. "I was at the school, working. Fixing her light – the ballast was going out. And then, I don't know…she was standing there."

Aaron smirked at him and Elijah just knew that he was holding back another round of laughter. He punched his older brother in the shoulder as hard as he could, because dammit all, he deserved it.

"Ow!" Aaron howled, rubbing at his shoulder. As a cop for the county, Aaron spent about as much time lifting weights as Elijah did mopping floors, so his shoulders were huge, muscles bulging everywhere. Eli didn't hurt him a bit and they both knew it. "What'd ya do that for?" Aaron demanded.

Eli ignored the question. "She can be pretty sometimes," he

announced. "When she isn't wearing her glasses," he added after a moment.

"I thought you were trying to decide whether or not she was pretty," Aaron reminded him.

"Well, maybe I've decided!" Elijah half-shouted and then settled back against his chair, taking another bite of his now-cold pizza while he scanned the ball pit for Brooksy and Juniper. There they were, having a ball fight and screeching up a storm the way only happy little girls could.

At least someone was having a good time.

He turned back to Aaron, who was staring at him with one eyebrow cocked. "What?" he asked defensively.

"You need to just ask her out already," Aaron said bluntly. "Go on a date with her, get a little action, and get her out of your system."

Easier said than done. As suave as Aaron was with girls, that's how godawful Elijah was with them. They were a terrifying group of human beings, no doubt about it.

"I...I don't know how to ask a girl out," he finally admitted. "I've only done it one time, and I ended up dating her for years and then being trapped into marriage. I don't exactly have a lot of experience with this. And what if Hannah ends up just like Sarah?"

"First of all," Aaron said in his best I'm-the-older-brother-so-I-know-everything voice that Eli absolutely detested, "Sarah is batshit crazy. Let's just get that out of the way. You can't go around thinking that every girl is going to end up like her. She's no measuring stick to measure shit by. And second of all, you ask Hannah out by asking her out."

*Helpful as always.*

"But...but there's Grindr and Tindr," Eli protested, "and people swiping left and right on their phones and I don't know...I don't know how to do any of that."

Aaron let out a sharp burst of laughter. "Brother, Grindr is for gay guys trying to find someone to hook up with. So unless there's something you need to tell me, you can skip that one. As for Tindr, that's how you meet the chick. You've already met Hannah. Now all that's left is to ask her out, bang her, get her out of your system, and move on with your life."

That was what Elijah needed to do, of course – one night of some hot 'n heavy sex and then move onto greener pastures – but still, hearing it being said out loud like that, so disrespectful…it rankled him.

He popped the last of his pizza crust into his mouth and chewed for a moment.

"I still don't know how," he finally admitted. "You just walk up to a girl and say, 'Hey, lady, wanna go see a movie with me?'"

"I'd try using her name instead of 'lady' but sure, that's the general idea."

Elijah glared at him. He didn't know what he'd been thinking, asking his brother for advice. Dumbest idea he'd ever come up with.

"You can always bring flowers or chocolates with you," Aaron added. "Girls like 'em. Ups the chances she'll say yes."

Eli brightened. Finally, a useful piece of advice. He knew Carla down at Happy Petals – she'd been a few graduating classes ahead of him, but she was the kind of person to always be damn nice to everyone. A body couldn't help but like Carla.

Yeah. He'd ask Carla for help – she'd know what to do.

# CHAPTER 14

## HANNAH

A MIDST THE HUSTLE and bustle of an overflowing Muffin Man, yet another meeting of the Early Spinster's Club came to order.

Which mostly just meant Hannah was picking at her healthy fruit-and-nut muffin, trying valiantly to convince herself that it tasted just as good as a donut would, while Michelle ate a chocolate-glazed donut with little sighs of ecstasy.

Hannah glared at her friend, which, of course, just made Michelle up the volume on her groans of pleasure to orgasmic levels.

*Why do I like her again?*

Before Hannah could decide if her choice of friends meant she was masochistic or not, Carla caught her eye. Bright blue eyes sparkling, she was bouncing up and down in her seat excitedly, which, to be honest, wasn't exactly earth-shattering news. Excitable and friendly to all, she was the most genuinely happy person Hannah had ever met. She'd chosen the store name of "Happy Petals" on purpose, after all, and never did a store name fit its owner better than that one did.

Finally, at her wit's end and incapable of listening to the ever-louder groans of happiness emanating from Michelle for one moment longer, Hannah pointedly asked Carla, "What're you so happy about?"

She took another dried-fruit-filled bite of her muffin and told herself that she liked it.

Which wasn't a lie. It was good. It just wasn't chocolate-glazed-donut good.

"I can't tell you," Carla said mysteriously, her whole body practically vibrating from the desire to do exactly that. "I can't break client-florist confidentiality." She bit down on her lower lip, and Hannah was sure she was trying to physically force herself not to say anything else.

Michelle stopped making groans of ecstasy long enough to burst out with, "What?" while Hannah was shaking her head at Carla and saying, "There is no such thing."

"There is, too," Carla said firmly, "and I'm not gonna break it. You just…keep your eyes peeled. That's all I'm saying."

Michelle understood what Carla was hinting at before Hannah did, and snatched Hannah's glasses off her face. Hannah made a wild grab for her glasses but Michelle held them easily out of reach, mostly because Hannah couldn't see well enough to know what she was grabbing at.

"What do you think?" Michelle asked Carla over Hannah's whispered pleas for her glasses back. "I'm thinking we oughta call Mor-Vision and see about getting Hannah into a pair of contacts."

The blob that was Carla moved around a bit in what Hannah imagined was a nodding motion. She was squinting as hard as she could, trying to bring the world around her into focus, even just a little, but it stayed the wavy, blurry mess it always was without her glasses on.

She made another wild swing at the Michelle blob, but came up with nothing. "Hi, Mrs. Mor," Hannah heard Michelle say sweetly.

*Man, she's fast. She must've had Mor-Vision on speed dial, just waiting for this opportunity.*

She wasn't exactly sure how she felt about that fact, honestly.

"I'm calling on behalf of Hannah Lambert," Michelle continued. "Does your husband have an opening anytime soon for her to get fitted with a pair of contacts?"

Hannah sank back into her chair, defeated. She felt naked as a blue jay without her glasses on to shield her from the world, and being blind as a bat to boot sure didn't help matters.

She glared at the Michelle blob as menacingly as she could.

"Sure thing, dear," said Mrs. Mor, her voice tinny through the phone speaker. "Your first appointment is here, Dr. Mor!" Hannah heard her yell, and then back to Michelle, just as sweet as pie, "We had a cancellation this morning so we have an opening at 4:15 today. Would that work?"

The Michelle blob was looking at Hannah, she just knew it. She nodded sullenly. Yeah, 4:15 would work. Didn't mean she had to like it, though.

"She says that'd be wonderful," Michelle said in a super cheerful voice. Hannah glared even harder. Suddenly, the super power of shooting death rays out of her eyeballs seemed like a completely awesome ability to have. "She'll see you then."

And then – finally! – Hannah's glasses were being slid back into her hands and she could put them on and see the world again. She sat back up, feeling better already. She glared at Michelle, who was grinning triumphantly, as Hannah took an overly large bite of her healthy muffin.

"Ummmm…ummmmm…" she groaned in fake ecstasy. If Michelle could do it, so could Hannah.

Sadly enough, though, Michelle just laughed at her.

*Hmph.*

Someday, Hannah was gonna get Michelle back for all of her teasing and ribbing.

Today just wasn't that day.

# CHAPTER 15

## ELIJAH

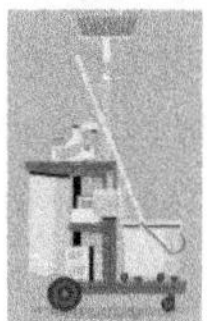

ELIJAH KNOCKED on the open door of Hannah's classroom, just like he did every afternoon, to announce his entrance into her world.

She looked up, just like she did every afternoon, to murmur a distracted hello before going back to work on whatever it was that she did after school.

Except, today wasn't like every other afternoon. Today, he had a bouquet of purple-and-white daisies underneath a dirty towel on top of his cleaning cart, ready to be revealed like some sort of janitorial version of a magic trick.

He began to push his cart into the room, but in shock, he stopped and stared instead.

Outta habit, Hannah had just gone to push the bridge of her glasses up her nose, except...there weren't any glasses to push up. She was apparently wearing contacts.

He was stuck in the doorway, staring at her, taking in the differences. Sure, she'd been pretty the other day when he'd pulled off her glasses, but she'd also been squinting up at him. Now that her glasses were gone but she could still see everything, he realized how big and gorgeous and blue her eyes were.

A mountain-lake-on-a-summer's-afternoon kinda blue.

His eyes dropped to her hands, which she was keeping hidden behind her desk, cradled in her lap. Was she fiddling with her fingers, all nervous? Was she just waiting for him to say something – to mention the change?

He wanted to speak, but blurting out, "You got yourself some contacts!" didn't seem real suave, so he pushed his cart into the room a little ways instead, hoping that if he was standing closer to her, maybe it wouldn't be so nerve-wracking to pull the towel off the cart.

He caught his breath as he got closer. She was staring up at him, still seated, her lower lip caught between her teeth as she waited for him to speak, but she looked…different somehow. More than just the glasses being gone, her whole face was different.

*Did she…did she have lipstick on?*

He took another step closer, trying to see.

He must've waited too long to say something, because she finally murmured, "I better get back to work," into the strained silence of the classroom, and dropped her eyes back down to her cluttered desk.

*Mascara.*

He'd be willing to bet next week's paycheck on the fact that she was wearing it today, and as far as he could remember, she'd never done that before. Not that he'd been staring at her eyeballs or something, but he also couldn't remember her lashes being that long or dark. They used to be this golden color, like the color of her hair but lighter. You had to be close to see them, but now, he could see 'em real easily.

*Not,* he reminded himself again, *that I've been staring at her eyes like a lovesick fool. I'm just an observant guy.*

The silence had stretched on too long. He needed to ask her out and get it over with.

"How's Brooksy been doing?" he blurted out, and immediately wanted to kick himself for it. Where on earth had that come from? "Uhhh…I mean, has she been kicking any boys lately?"

"No, she's doing much better," Hannah said, looking back up at him, her face lighting up from having something to talk to him about. "And her clothes…she's coming to school with clothes that look new, and that actually fit her. Did you talk to Sarah about it?"

"Yeah, we had a discussion," Elijah grumbled, getting pissed off all over again when he remembered *that* conversation. Sarah's words had been all slurry as they'd talked, and he'd been damn sure during the whole conversation that she wouldn't remember what they'd talked about come morning.

He'd asked her what'd happened to the clothes she was supposed to be buying for Brooksy with that $200 he'd practically killed himself to give her, and she'd hemmed and hawed around the question for a good five minutes before finally admitting that she'd gone makeup shopping with it.

"I looked at her clothes, and they were fine," she'd told him as snotty as could be. It hadn't come out how she'd planned, though; she'd had a hard time pronouncing "clothes" and had added an extra syllable into it: *clothezes*. Even for her, this was a new level of drunk.

"No, they aren't," Elijah had bit out. He'd wanted to tear into her – how *dare* she make him pay his truck payment late just so she could have some fancy-ass makeup – but from past experience, he knew there was no point.

It was better to focus on Brooksy and how Sarah's actions had hurt their daughter. Or, more to the point, how Sarah's actions had made Sarah look bad, which was really all that she cared about.

"Brooksy split her pants at recess yesterday. Do you want everyone to think that she comes from a poor white trash family?"

He'd dug the knife in right where it hurt Sarah the most, and hadn't felt the least bit bad about it. If all Sarah cared about was appearances, then by God, he'd use that to get Brooksy what she needed. Sarah had always made fun of the way Eli talked; had wanted the best of everything; had made him feel like a loser 'cause she wasn't driving a new car each year.

Calling her white trash was the worst thing you could say to her, and Eli enjoyed doing it a little too much.

Sarah had been silent for a moment, and then he'd heard the muffled sound of her covering up the phone and demanding of Brooksy, "Did you split your pants at school?" He hadn't been able to hear her answer but sure enough, Sarah had came back on the line and had snapped, "We'll go shopping tomorrow," before hanging up the phone.

No apology, no excuses.

Anyone who expected something else from Sarah would be sorely disappointed. He'd learned that a long time ago.

"Well, it's sure made a huge difference," Hannah said brightly, bringing Elijah back to the present. And back to the part where he had flowers hidden underneath the dirty towel on top of his cart. As he looked at the cart, the flowers seemed blazingly obvious, something a blind person wouldn't miss. What else would cause such a bizarre-shaped lump right there on top?

But Hannah hadn't so much as looked at it since he wheeled his cart into the room.

He opened up his mouth, sucked in a deep breath, and yanked the dirty towel off his cart while blurting out in one breath, "Will-you-date-me?" He grabbed the bouquet of daisies and shoved them at her, over top the piles on her desk, into her hands that she'd been keeping hidden there.

Hannah took 'em slowly, looking down at the bouquet and back up at him to ask, "Date you?"

"Well, go on a date," he clarified.

"And where would you take me to, on this date?"

"Uhhh…"

Which was when his brain froze, of course, offering up absolutely nothing.

He'd been thinking beforehand 'bout a couple of different places but hadn't managed to pick one yet.

Now, all of those places and any other place on the planet other than Hannah's classroom seemed to have completely disappeared from his mind, as if none of them existed. "As long as you're with me, I don't rightly care where," he finally admitted.

"What a romantic," Hannah teased him lightly as she brought the flowers up to her face to breathe in their smell.

He scowled at her. "It's not romantic – it's practical," he protested.

"It's a good thing to be a romantic," she told him seriously.

*Huh. Sure. Girls are so weird sometimes.*

"I'd love to go on a date with you...somewhere," Hannah said, serious as a heart attack but her eyes...they were glinting with mischief.

Had she always had this teasing side to her and he'd just missed it behind those coke-bottle glasses?

"The glasses...thing..." He waved his hand in the general direction of her face. "It looks good. Mighty good."

What he really, really wanted in that moment was for the ground to swallow him up. Talking to a woman was proving to be just as difficult as he'd thought it was gonna be.

And he hadn't exactly thought it was gonna go real smooth.

"Thank you," she said softly, smiling up at him. She had a real pretty smile, with small, straight, square teeth, not oversized and overlapping in the front like his. He'd always been self-conscious about his smile because of the overlap and because of how big his teeth were – he felt like a horse sometimes, with teeth way too large to fit in his head. Hannah's were just perfect. Made him wanna make her smile at him again.

"So, I'll see you on Friday. Six-thirty. At your dad's house?"

She nodded, still smiling slightly at him.

"Good, good." He backed up, pulling his cart with him, his magic trick over for the moment. "I'll…uhh…see you then."

"Um, before you leave," she called out, stopping him before he could escape down the hallway, "could you empty my trash cans? They got a bit full today."

*Shhhhiiitttttt…*

He felt the red creep up his neck again as he nodded and hurried towards the two trash cans she had out around her room. It was the whole reason why he'd been in her classroom, after all – at least according to the school district – but he'd completely lost his mind and had forgotten all about his job.

The thing that kept him from being homeless and starving. *That* thing.

Trash emptied, he hurried outta the classroom and down the hallway, deciding that he'd sweep and mop her floors later. Preferably when she wasn't anywhere near the building.

He was done making an ass of himself, at least for today.

# CHAPTER 16

## HANNAH

Hannah watched in the mirror as Carla carefully brushed her cheeks with some sort of rouge. She was having Carla do her makeup yet again, which made her feel a little worthless, like a small child who couldn't take care of herself. When she'd confessed that to Carla, she'd just replied with a laugh that she loved to do it, which made Hannah both roll her eyes and sigh with envy at the same time.

Of *course* she did. Carla did this sort of thing effortlessly – lots of makeup, lots of jewelry, lots of colorful clothes. She always included her signature turquoise somewhere in the outfit, which she would then pair with another bright color – pink or lime green or a brilliant purple. Somehow, instead of looking like she was an escaped clown from the insane asylum like Hannah would with that much going on, Carla had this amazing ability to make it look good.

She reminded Hannah of a colorful bird from the tropics – flitting and fluttering about, always on the move, always gorgeous. Sure, she was a little heavier than the stick-thin models that *Vogue* put on their covers, but if a guy could just see past that, Hannah was sure he'd agree that Carla was the most beautiful woman around. Hannah had always secretly envied her friend's long, dark hair that she styled into waves down her back, like a rippling, shimmering sheet caught in a gentle wind.

"I really should learn how to do this," Hannah murmured without a drop of sincerity as Carla put some final touches on her hair with a curling iron, brandishing it as skillfully as a swordsman with a rapier. She had to admit that having her hair down, the red curls spilling everywhere, was a lot more flattering than having her hair pulled straight back into a strict bun. Then again, she hadn't wanted to be beautiful before now, so it wasn't exactly a struggle to up the bar in the looks department.

"Pshaw," Carla said dismissively, "and take away all of my fun?" She stepped back to admire her handiwork, her hands on her broad hips as she studied Hannah in the mirror. "He's not gonna believe his eyes when he sees you tonight," she pronounced with excitement.

Hannah looked back at the bathroom mirror, her mouth twisting in disbelief. She did have to admit that she looked… different. She wasn't sure if she liked war paint or not, though, and that was all she could think of when she saw this much makeup on a person: They were getting ready to go to war.

Without Hannah even saying a word, Carla laughed at her. "You do not look like an Indian about to go to war," she said, her bright blue eyes crinkling with amusement. "You look beautiful."

Hannah stuck her tongue out at Carla. It was perhaps possible that she'd used the war paint analogy more than once with her friend.

Just possible.

There was a loud knock on the front door, startling them both. Carla looked at her, excitement stamped all over her face. "It's him!" she announced in a whisper-squeal that only Carla could produce. "I'll just let myself out the back door." She hurried and gathered up her things, heading for the door before turning back to whisper, "I want to hear every detail at the next meeting. Every one of them," and with that, she shut the door behind her quietly, slipping through the backyard and out into the alleyway where she'd stealthily parked her turquoise van with HAPPY PETALS emblazoned on it for a quick getaway.

Hannah pulled at her above-the-knee skirt – normally something she never, ever wore, but Carla had absolutely insisted she put on because, "It shows off your legs," as she bluntly put it – and then walked as sedately as she could towards the front door, forcing herself not to race over. She hadn't been this excited about a date in…never, actually.

Never, ever, ever.

Despite her best efforts, her breath was coming in short gasps by time she opened the door. She wouldn't pass out. She wouldn't. That would be embarrassing, to say the least.

So she just wouldn't.

And then she opened the door to find Mr. Morland standing there, looking way more handsome than she had any idea he could look, and he'd already been handsome before, and…

Her vision darkened a bit around the edges and she wondered if she could faint gracefully or if she'd be one of those people who crumpled to a heap on the floor, hitting her head on the way down and waking up in the hospital with a giant white bandage wrapped around her head.

That would just be her luck.

The ridiculousness of the scenario playing out in her mind pulled her away from the heat of her thoughts long enough for the danger to pass, so she was able to look up at him with a smile instead of with an, "Oh my!" and a Scarletesque faint.

"Hello," he said with a smile, and then all talking stopped as he drank in the sight of her.

She'd never been so thoroughly looked over before – she was used to blending into the background. In fact, it was what she tried to do. If given even a quarter of a chance, she'd melt into the hustle and bustle of life and no one would ever think twice about her.

It was what she'd always wanted.

But now…

Having Elijah Morland look at her like she was laid out for him on a platter? As if she was the most beautiful woman he'd ever laid eyes on?

Turned out, she didn't mind being noticed after all.

"I didn't know…you're…wow." He stuttered to a stop and just stared at her for a moment longer. "Hannah, you're beautiful," he finally got out.

She ducked her head, letting the curls of bright auburn hair hide her flaming cheeks for a moment. They were a brilliant red, and not from the blush that Carla had so liberally applied.

"Thanks," she said softly. She studied him through her eyelashes, letting her gaze travel from his well worn but polished shoes, up his black slacks – she didn't even know he owned slacks – and to the open collar of his shirt. He'd actually worn a button-up shirt tonight, also something she didn't know he owned.

*Isn't Elijah just full of all sorts of surprises…*

The thought caught her up short.

When, exactly, had she stopped thinking of him as Mr. Morland, and had started thinking of him as Elijah? She searched back in her mind, but couldn't remember.

This was dangerous, of course. He was the father of a student.

She absolutely, positively shouldn't be doing it.

Of course, she also absolutely, positively shouldn't be going on a date with him, so…

"Ready to go?" she asked, ignoring every clanging warning bell going off in her head.

For once, she'd live dangerously. Never mind that she didn't have a rebellious bone in her body. She could pretend, right?

Just for tonight?

He held his arm out for her and she slipped hers into his, feeling the rush and tingle of being so close to a sexy man.

No, she shouldn't be doing this at all. Which was probably why she was so thrilled by it.

He helped her into his diesel truck that looked old enough to have been the personal transportation for Noah before Noah had gotten around to building an ark, but once inside, she found that it was shockingly clean. No stray dog hair or dirt clumps or old soda bottles or crumpled receipts; it looked like it had just come off the showroom floor.

As he turned the key and then waited for the glow plugs to warm up, she said sincerely, "I'm really impressed by how clean you keep your truck. No wonder you make such a good janitor." Maybe she was a dork to be impressed by something like this, but she couldn't help herself. He was certainly better about keeping his vehicle clean than she was about hers. Usually, she had stacks of things everywhere – stacks to go into her house. Stacks to go into her classroom. Stacks to go to the office of the school. Stacks to go everywhere else in town.

And that wasn't even counting the miscellaneous trash that always seemed to pile up while she wasn't looking.

The warning light for the glow plugs turned off and he started the truck, the rumble of the diesel vibrating straight through her as he turned to look at her. "It's normally a disaster zone," he admitted cheerfully with a shrug of his shoulders. "But I thought I oughta clean it up for tonight's date."

Somehow, that was an even bigger compliment than the comment about her beauty. The fact that he would take the time; that this date was a big enough deal to him to do that…

She snuck in another pinch of her arm, wanting to make sure this wasn't some glorious dream.

*Ouch!*

Nope, definitely not a dream.

"So, did you decide where 'somewhere' would be for our date?" she asked teasingly as they began to head in the general direction of Franklin. A part of her was sad that they weren't making the drive to Boise – which lay in the opposite direction from Franklin – if only because then they wouldn't be in a car together for hours on end. Unlike Boise, the drive to Franklin was a mere thirty minutes away.

She wanted this night to never, no *never* stop.

He took a right onto the highway, his headlights piercing through the gathering twilight to show the way. "You know Villano's?" he asked rhetorically. "It's Brooksy's favorite place to go for dinner, and hell, their pizza is divine, even if the cook loses your order half the time."

"They do?" she said, surprised. She'd not heard that before, but then again, she wasn't normally the one that people made sure to tell every last piece of information to. She wasn't exactly the gossip queen of Sawyer, that was for sure.

"Long story," he said dryly. "Anyway, I thought it'd be fun, and hopefully since it's not a Saturday afternoon, there won't be piles of shrieking children climbing all over the jungle gym and ball pit."

At that, her stomach sank and shrunk into a bundle of nerves, tumbling and twirling endlessly inside of her. *Now* she remembered Villano's. She wasn't someone to go out to eat very often – a teacher's salary didn't allow for many extravagances, and just the coffee and muffins she bought during the meetings of the Early Spinster's Club from the Muffin Man was stretching it – but she'd gone there once, with her dad. Before he...

Well anyway, Elijah was right – it was a pizza parlor with a ball pit and a jungle gym. Sure, it was adorable that he chose restaurants based on where his daughter liked to eat, but this... this was a recipe for disaster. The chances were roughly 100% or so that she'd know at least one child in the place, if not half of them.

She'd wanted to slide in under the radar; she'd wanted to keep a low profile and not have anyone notice that she was breaking every rule in the teacher handbook, and then some extra ones just for funsies.

A pizza parlor with a ball pit? Not the way to make that happen.

She sank down in her seat, anxiety overwhelming her. This beautiful, amazing, once-in-a-lifetime date was turning into a disaster real quick. But the idea of being brave enough to tell Elijah no, to say that she wanted to do something else...what if he told her never mind, I don't want to go on a date with you after all? What if he turned around and dropped her off at home and drove away?

She couldn't bear the thought.

She sunk further down into her seat, wishing for anything to save her – anything in the world. Tornado, earthquake, the Yellowstone super volcano erupting...

And still, the miles ticked by with nature blissfully at peace.

# CHAPTER 17

## ELIJAH

THEY PULLED UP to Villano's and Eli quickly jumped out and hurried around to Hannah's side, wanting to help her out like a gentleman would. He might come from the wrong side of the tracks, but he didn't want Hannah to know it.

Okay, so she already knew it – they both grew up in Sawyer, so hiding his background wasn't exactly an option – but maybe she didn't remember. And if she did, maybe she wasn't thinking about it tonight.

But as he held his hand up to her to help her out, she just sat stubbornly in her seat, shaking her head frantically, her dark red curls going everywhere from the force of the shaking.

"I can't go in there," she whispered, the panic as clear as day in her voice. He stared at her, the fact that she was sitting in his truck making 'em eye to eye for once.

*The easier to kiss her…*

He pushed the stray thought away.

"What's wrong? Are you…are you one of those gluten-free people?" He couldn't help the accusing tone in his voice. If she knew she was gluten free, why, she could've told him anywhere along the way. She'd said hardly a word since they left Sawyer; it wasn't like she didn't have 30 minutes of opportunity to share this little tidbit with him.

She shook her head. "No, I'm good friends with gluten."

Silence.

"But you're not gonna go into the pizza parlor with me," he said, stating the obvious, hoping she'd contradict him and jump out of the truck to trail after him.

Silence.

"I just…well, you see, I'm breaking about 25 school district rules by sitting here with you, and going on a date with you, and I was hoping that we'd go some place without kids, and without a lot of other adults, and then no one would know that I'm breaking the rules because I'm not a rule breaker except in this case but I was hoping not to get caught since I'm just breaking the rules this one time." The tsunami of words finally stopped and she drew in a deep breath. "So, I can't go inside with you. See?"

He thought that Brooksy could really talk a blue streak when she got on a roll, but that…Hannah had just put his daughter to shame.

He tried to think back through what'd just spilled out of her. *Not a rule-breaker? Isn't that what rules are there for – so you can break them? They're not there so you can actually follow them, right?*

He stared at her. She stared at him.

She looked positively freaked out.

What he oughta do was get back in the truck and drive Hannah home. She knew it; he knew it. Despite being from the same tiny town in the middle of Nowhere, Idaho, they had exactly nothing else in common. Why, she probably didn't even like country music. Or beer. Or spending time down at the shootin' range.

"Who is your favorite country singer?" he demanded.

"Who is my favorite?" she repeated, staring at him as if he'd lost his mind. He stared back, not moving an inch. *If she says Faith Hill, I'm driving her ass back home. She is not a real country singer.*

"Ummm…probably Alabama. I know they're a little older but their stuff from the 90s…" She shrugged. "Their songs always have a story to them."

He nodded begrudgingly. Alabama did put out some good stuff. "Fine. What kinda beer do you drink?"

Her mouth dropped open as she stared at him. He could practically see the wheels turn in her head as she tried to figure out where the hell he was going with this line of questioning.

"I prefer red wine," she started out, and he exclaimed, "Aha!" in triumph.

"But if I'm given just beer to choose from," she continued on as if he'd said nothing at all, "then I'd go with a Coors."

"Coors Light?" he challenged her. *Shit, that ain't nothin' but colored water.*

"No, Coors," she corrected him politely. "If I'm going to drink beer, then I want to drink the real stuff."

*Huh.*

Now he was back to staring at her.

She'd passed his tests, and had done it calmly while he'd been doing nothing but acting like a jackass to her. There she was with her dark red hair and her pretty blue eyes and wearing lipstick and wearing a skirt that fit real nice, and all he could do was be a dick.

He felt awful.

And then inspiration struck.

"I've got it!" he said, and headed back around to his side of the truck. He couldn't afford to take her to some fancy restaurant – Villano's was gonna be a stretch on his budget – but he could always cook a meal for her at home. He wasn't what he'd consider to be a chef or something, but he knew a few dishes real good.

"Where are we going?" Hannah asked as he backed out into the street, clearly worried that he was just gonna pick another child-filled restaurant for them to eat at.

He shot her a grin. "Home. I promise you, there aren't any children there, and the only parent you'll find is me. I don't normally see much reason to get fancy for just Brooksy and me, but I know a coupla dishes that you might enjoy. I bagged a deer this fall, so I got plenty of deer meat I can cook up." He looked at her challengingly. "Unless you got something against eating Bambi."

She swallowed hard, her face going a little pale at the question. "I can't say that I consciously try to think that I'm eating Bambi," she allowed, "but I don't have a problem with eating deer in general. In fact, I think that killing your own animals and eating them makes you more in tune with it all." She waved her hand around the cab of the truck. "If the only meat you ever eat comes from the grocery store in a styrofoam container wrapped up in plastic, you just might start to forget that there was ever an animal involved in the process."

He had a hard time seeing her face in the dim lighting of the cab, the sun having long ago set, but still he squinted through the darkness at her, trying to spot if she was serious. She looked like she was, which went a long way in making him feel better.

"That's how I've always looked at it, too," he said softly, a little surprised that their views were similar. He hadn't thought he'd have much in common with Hannah – he'd asked her out 'cause she was cute and like Aaron had said, he just needed to get her out of his system. He hadn't expected to actually like her.

"So tell me about your family," Hannah said encouragingly. "I know Aaron, of course, since we graduated the same year, but somehow, I don't remember ever meeting your parents."

He gripped the steering wheel hard, wishing for the miles to go by faster. Was it really another 25 minutes before they'd make it back to Sawyer? He'd be hard-pressed to pretend deafness for the entire drive.

He sighed.

"My parents are…interesting," he finally settled on saying. "They aren't your typical parents." He shut up then, hoping she'd take the hint and leave the topic the hell alone.

But Hannah was a girl, and that meant – along with all of her fun curves – came the inability to leave shit alone.

"'Not typical'?" she repeated. "In what way?"

"In the 'we should love our children but don't' way," he said harshly, and then instantly regretted it. It wasn't Hannah's fault that his parents were so screwed up. But the reason why they didn't love him…well, it would probably be the reason why Hannah wouldn't either. It was time to lay his cards all out on the table and scare her the hell off.

It was only right.

"I knocked up my girlfriend the summer after high school graduation," he said baldly. He snuck a look at her out of the corner of his eye, and found that she was just looking at him steadily, waiting for him to continue.

Not what he was expecting, but it gave him enough courage to keep going. Tell her the truth most people had guessed, but he'd never confirmed.

"Sarah didn't tell me that she'd stopped taking her birth control pills. She'd wanted to get married, and I'd told her that we were too young. I was gonna go to college and make something of myself. She thought that since we were out of high school, that we were adults and so we were old enough to get married. She doesn't…" He blew out a breath. "She don't take no for an answer. Like, ever. I should've realized something was wrong when she stopped bringing up marriage every other sentence. Just a couple of months later, she was preggers with Brooksy."

He paused, wanting to change topics and talk about something else – anything else – but somehow, he already knew

Hannah well enough to know that she'd circle back to this topic at some point. She was more subtle than Sarah, that was for damn sure, but there was a streak of stubbornness in her a mile wide.

"What does this have to do with your parents?" Hannah asked softly when his pause had apparently gone on too long.

They were nearing the lights of Sawyer, and Elijah was already breathing a little easier. Soon, they'd be at his place and he could find something different to talk about. Them making dinner together. How Brooksy was doing in school. The position of Jupiter.

Anything at all except for this.

"I was never their favorite," he finally said. "Aaron had his shit together. Still does. Being the golden child and all, he graduated from high school and went straight to college for six years to get his degree in Criminology. He'd known since he was little that he wanted to be a cop when he grew up, and that he was gonna be the police chief someday. He's still working on that last part, of course." Elijah chuckled at that, and then continued, "I'd always wanted to be...well, never mind. So there was Aaron at college, getting good grades, working a part-time job to make it through without racking up lots of debt, and meanwhile, I'm struggling to keep my head above water in high school. You oughta know – I'm the dumb one in the family. My dad says that I was dropped on my head lots as a kid, and now it shows."

He laughed humorlessly.

Hannah didn't.

She wasn't moving or speaking at all, just watching him in the darkness and listening to him talk. He'd think that she'd fallen asleep on him, except he could see the light catch her eyes every once in a while and he knew she was still looking at him.

He pulled up in front of his ramshackle house and cut the engine. The rumble of the diesel died away, leaving just the two of them in the darkness.

He realized with a start that it was easier to talk to her when he couldn't see her face, so he plunged on, wanting to get the story over and done with, never to be mentioned again.

"My parents told me that if I was old enough to knock a girl up, then I was old enough to take care of her. They frog-marched me down to the courthouse and I got married to Sarah lickety-split, almost before I knew what was going on. After that, they cut all support. Life was hard? Couldn't pay my bills? Well, it's what I deserved for getting a girl in the family way. They're real religious, and the idea that their son was having sex before he was married…they were pissed, all right.

"Sarah, on the other hand, was happy as a clam since she got what she wanted, but soon, that wore off. She'd wanted to get married and play house; she hadn't wanted to actually *be* married. You know, the hard stuff. After Brooksy was born, there were late-night feedings and stinky diapers – none of it was how she'd thought it'd be. I don't know what she thought, but whatever it was, she sure was wrong. We were both kids and didn't have a damn clue of what we were doing.

"As for Brooksy…my parents don't like her. Oh, they pretend – they send a five-dollar bill on her birthday and another one at Christmas, and they sign the cards 'Love, the Morlands,' like they were the neighbors or something, instead of her grandparents. Aaron hasn't had any kids, so this is their only grandchild. I think they have a closer relationship to the kids at the church they go to on Sunday. Since I wasn't married to Sarah when I knocked her up, Brooksy isn't good enough for my parents. They're waiting for Aaron the Perfect to get married so they can love on his kids."

He trailed off then, nothing else to say.

They were sitting in his truck, staring straight ahead at the garage door, neither of them speaking, the croak of frogs the only sound breaking the silence. He didn't want to look at Hannah and see the judgment in her eyes. It was a small town, so she'd probably already guessed that Brooksy was a bastard child – at least before he married Sarah – but maybe she'd forgotten.

Well, she remembered now.

*Stupid Elijah, telling her all of that. Stupid, stupid. Shoulda kept quiet. She's never gonna wanna date you now—*

"Your parents are idiots," she said firmly, as if it'd been up to her to judge their abilities as parents, and she'd made the final decision on the topic. "Brooklyn is one of my most endearing, smart, loving, and precocious children in my class. If your parents are too close-minded to take the time to know her, then they don't deserve her."

*Precocious.* He turned the word around and around in his mind, trying to figure out what in the hell it meant. He vowed to himself to look it up after Hannah went home. He'd already told her that he was the stupid one; he didn't need to prove it to her.

"I'm sorry to hear all of that," she said softly, laying a hand on his arm. Warm tingles shot through him at her touch and he finally turned to look at her. Her red hair looked black in the darkness, and almost without thought, he reached out to run his fingers through it. It was as soft as it looked, and at his touch, she turned her face into his hand and nuzzled his palm.

The world stopped in that moment. He couldn't hardly breathe, having a pretty lady like Hannah Lambert liking him. Shit like that just didn't happen to a dummy from the wrong side of the tracks.

He forced himself to pull away. "We should get to cooking," he said softly. "Our trip to Franklin and back for no good reason is gonna make this dinner later than normal anyhow."

"I'm sorr—"

He cut her off, placing a calloused finger on her soft lips. The electricity was sparking so strong between them, it was likely to set his truck on fire if he wasn't careful.

He wasn't real sure he wanted to be careful.

"I should've thought of it," he admitted. "I'm so used to

choosing based on what Brooksy likes, it didn't even occur to me."

Before she could change her mind and tell him that she wanted to go home after all, he slid out of the truck and over to her side to help her out.

He wasn't about to let Miss Hannah Lambert go home.

Not yet, anyway.

# CHAPTER 18

## HANNAH

HANNAH TRAILED ELIJAH slightly as they walked into his house, making it easy for her to catch the slight tightening of his shoulders as they went through the beat-up front door. He looked more nervous than a long-tailed cat in a room full of rocking chairs, and as she looked around his well-worn home, she was pretty sure she knew why.

He'd cleaned out his truck, knowing she'd be riding in it, but he hadn't planned on taking her back to his house. He probably didn't think it was clean enough for her or something.

She put her hand on his arm – a move that took way too much courage but she forced herself to do it anyway – and said, "It looks fine, really. You weren't expecting me to see it, so of course it didn't get the spit 'n shine treatment that the truck did."

He laughed a little at that. "Don't be giving away my janitor secrets so easily," he mock-scolded her. "You can't go 'round telling everybody that I add a little spit to every cleaning. They might take over my job and then where would I be?" He laughed derisively at the idea, and she chuckled politely even as she wondered again what he actually wanted to do as a career. He'd started to tell her in the truck but had changed topics mid-sentence, making her sure that there was something there.

Something he wasn't willing to share with her just yet.

Before she could figure out a discreet way of probing him, though, he led the way into a threadbare kitchen; scuff marks, entrenched dirt, and even a few deep gashes showing the age of the half-century-old orange-and-brown linoleum floors. The drab olive green Formica countertops had seen more than a few hot pans set directly down on it, and no amount of scrubbing was ever going to bring it back to life.

"I was thinking we could—" He stopped when he saw her gaze was focused on the extreme divots in the floor. "It's a rental," he said by way of explanation. "The best I could afford on a janitor's income and my ex sucking up every last penny she can."

"Why don't you show me what I can do to help with dinner," she said politely, hoping that understanding was showing in her eyes, and not pity. A man like Elijah wouldn't want pity. "I'm not the world's best cook but I do know which end of the knife to hold, so there's that."

He laughed and the tension in his shoulders eased just a little. "Sounds like you and me have about the same cooking skills," he said with an endearing grin that was a perfect match to Brooklyn's. "I haven't burned down my kitchen yet, so I figure I'm doing real good." He shrugged and they set about cooking.

He had her work on a simple salad while he defrosted two deer steaks. The white wrapping around the meat, along with the stamp proclaiming "Kendall's Kuts" on the side, made it obvious that it was cut and wrapped down at the local butcher shop.

"You have Kurt Kendall cut and wrap for you?" she asked, a little surprised as she got to work on dicing tomatoes. "I thought he mostly focused on domestic animals, like pig and cow."

Elijah sent her a shocked look. "You're right, of course, but he's a good friend of mine, so he does my deer and elk on the side. I can't believe you know which butcher in town does which kinda animal."

It was her turn to laugh. "First off, I taught three of Mr. Kendall's kids, so I know him and his wife real well. Second of all, my dad liked to hunt and would take me along, both to the hunting part and to the butchering part. He said it would teach me to appreciate my food. Before, you know…" She waved her hand around the general area of her head, hoping she wouldn't have to say anything more.

At Eli's confused look he shot her over his shoulder, she finished quietly, a huge lump in her throat. "Before he forgot who I am, and how to turn a key in a lock."

"He doesn't remember how to use a key?" Elijah asked incredulously. He was heating up a cast iron skillet as they chatted, and the fact that he wasn't looking at her made it a little easier for her to talk. *Please don't look at me. Please don't look at me.* She twisted a lock of her hair around and around in her fingers. She was more relaxed around Elijah than she was any other adult who didn't belong to the Early Spinster's Club, but that didn't mean that she was actually relaxed.

She mostly felt like her stomach was doing its best to trade places with her heart, and her heart wasn't going along with it.

"That was the first real sign of dementia for him." She forced herself to pull her fingers out of her hair and focused instead on the head of lettuce Elijah had handed to her. She made sure it came out in even strips, not a cut out of place. "Before that, he'd forget about appointments or would stumble over my name – stupid stuff that everyone does. I was a little worried about him, but I think everyone worries about their parents getting older and being able to take care of themselves. I told myself that I was mother-henning him to death, so I needed to give him space. I had myself convinced that the fact that he sometimes would forget that my mom was gone was practically normal. And then…"

The strips of lettuce were becoming increasingly thinner and more precise, starting to resemble linguini noodles rather than lettuce for a salad but the movement was soothing and she couldn't seem to stop herself.

Here was something she could control.

*Slice…slice…slice…*

Elijah wasn't talking and for once, silence was actually bothering Hannah, and so she filled the void.

"I stopped by one day to check on him, and found him on the front porch, upset as could be. It took a while to figure out what was going on, because of course he didn't know what was going on, only that he couldn't get into his house. I kept telling him to put the key in the lock and it was like he didn't understand the English language anymore. The words had no meaning to him."

Her throat closed up and she swallowed hard, trying to push down the panic she'd felt that day when she'd finally been forced to realize that her father, the strongest man she knew, was sliding into a deep, dark hole that she couldn't help him out of.

"I showed him…" The world was going wavy around her and her eyes were hot and she was trying not to cry; trying not to show how her whole world had fallen to pieces in an instant.

She wasn't weak; she was strong.

She had to be. For her dad.

"I showed him how," she started again, past the grapefruit-sized lump in her throat, "to put the key into the lock and turn it, and he kept shaking his head and saying it was too hard. He couldn't do it. Locks were the first thing to go, but he quickly lost other abilities, too, like how to run a microwave or how to put on a belt. They were simple, stupid, *stupid* things and he just…couldn't."

The lettuce was a mushy mess in front of her and still she

was slicing, and then Eli's hand was on her shoulder and he was pulling her into his arms, wrapping them snuggly around her, holding her and shielding her from the world where she had to be the parent and her dad was the child. She sobbed into his shirt, the sound of her heart rushing in her ears and she couldn't breathe or think but only cry and then cry some more.

After an eternity or two, the pain began to subside along with the tide of tears, and she pulled back with a watery smile. "I bet you've never had a date bawl on you like that before," she said ruefully, swiping at her eyes, trying to keep from smearing her makeup even more than she already had. All of Carla's hard work, destroyed in an instant.

The thought made her confront the fact that she'd made a real fool out of herself. She felt her cheeks stain red as she pulled further away, embarrassed as a teen caught making out with her boyfriend, and she felt a different panic well up inside of her. She'd not had much experience dating guys – none worth speaking about, anyway – but even she knew that bawling like a baby and smearing makeup everywhere wasn't exactly the way to ensure a second date.

She began blindly stumbling away, in search of a bathroom where she could splash cold water on her face and clean off her destroyed makeup, when she felt Elijah's hand on her. "Hold still," he said soothingly, tilting her head up to look him straight in the eye as he began to wipe her face with a Kleenex. She couldn't bear to keep eye contact with him while he did such an embarrassing task, so she settled on keeping her eyes closed and letting him clean her up like he would a small child.

"Did you learn how to do this with Brooklyn?" she asked, keeping her eyes closed, hoping that the ostrich method of dealing with embarrassing events really did work.

"Yeah," he said softly, turning her face gently in the palm of his calloused, work-roughened hand. "You can't raise a 10-year-old girl without more than a few breakdowns. As a fifth grade teacher, I'm sure you know just what I'm talking about."

She cringed inwardly. "It's true," she said with an embarrassed chuckle. She began to wonder if crawling underneath his bed and hiding for the rest of the night was an option or not. "Although boys tend to work things out with their fists, they have more than their fair share of crying bouts, too."

"Looking good," Elijah said softly, and she forced her eyes open to look up at him. She didn't want to – Lord knew she didn't – but somehow, she was just sure that was what he was waiting for, and he wouldn't move an inch until she did.

"You're one of the prettiest girls I've ever seen," he whispered. "What're you doing with an idiot like me?"

And then he was kissing her, his mouth moving hungrily over hers, pressing and probing his tongue against the seam of her lips, seeking entry into her mouth. She didn't know what she was doing – the list of men who'd ever kissed her only had one man on it, and she definitely didn't want to put Elijah into *that* camp – but she did her best to follow his lead by opening up. He groaned against her lips as his tongue swept inside, setting parts of her ablaze that she hadn't paid attention to in a very long time. She instinctively dug her fingers into his muscular shoulders, trying to regain her balance in a suddenly tilting world.

No, this definitely wasn't like the other time she'd been kissed. Not at all. This was glorious, amazing, gravity-defying—

It was the burning smell that brought them back to reality.

One moment, she was lost in a world that she hadn't known existed and never wanted to leave, and the next, her nose was twitching, and so was his. They pulled back and stared at each other for a second going onto a millennium before they both spun towards the stove. There, smoking, were the deer steaks, little tendrils curling up from them like miniature smoke signals.

"Shit!" Elijah roared as he grabbed a hot pad and yanked the cast iron pan off the gas burner, staring down at the ruined meat with a look of total horror.

Hannah looked down at the pan too, and suddenly, giggles overtook her. She shouldn't be laughing – she knew she shouldn't – but she just couldn't help herself.

He glowered at her darkly, clearly not seeing the humor in the situation. "You have to admit," she said around another bout of laughter, "that this is a dandy of a compliment." She gestured towards the smoking, ruined deer steaks.

"Compliment?" He stared at her like she'd lost her mind.

And maybe she had. Tonight's date had been anything but dull. Maybe the stress of it all was causing her to go a little nuts in the head.

"Well," she said slowly, not wanting to admit to insanity quite yet, "I like to think that kissing me was such an amazing experience, you completely lost track of where you were and what you were doing. That's a heck of a kiss, right?"

First, one side of his mouth twitched, and then the other side twitched. His eyes started glowing, and then the laughter came roaring out. "I like how you think!" he said, wiping at his eyes when he was finally done laughing. "That kind of optimism...I sure could use a dose or two of it in my life."

She batted her eyelashes at him. "I do my best," she told him mock seriously.

Honestly, she tended to be more of a realist than an optimist. Life could be downright crappy at times, and she just didn't have it in her to always look for the bright side of every awful event.

But two burnt steaks? It wasn't hard to find the humor in that.

"So," he said, growing serious and staring down at the massacred slabs of meat, "that was my idea for dinner. I'm striking out all over the place."

She shrugged. "You have easy kid food, right? Canned soup and bread to make grilled sandwiches?"

"But, we're on a date," he protested.

"And a wise man once told me that all that mattered was being with each other," she said with a wink. She couldn't believe that she had the cojones to tease a guy like this, but there was something endearing and not too terribly intimidating about Elijah Morland, even if he was a guy, and even if he was handsome as sin.

He grinned at her. "He does sound like an awfully wise guy," he said with a laugh. "We oughta listen to him."

"My thoughts exactly. Now, where is the canned soup hiding?"

# CHAPTER 19

## ELIJAH

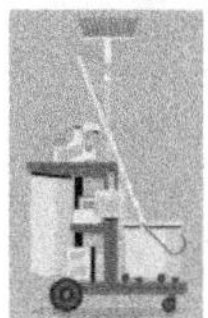

AFTER THEY SAT DOWN to the most childish, least inspiring meal ever served on a date – Campbell's soup and grilled cheese sandwiches weren't exactly gonna set anyone's hair on fire with delight – Elijah tried to think of something to talk about.

*Teaching. Everyone likes talking about their careers.*

*Everyone who has a career, that is.*

He pushed that thought away.

"What made you decide to be a teacher?" he asked, watching her neatly cut her sandwich into two triangles and then dip one of the corners into the soup. Awkwardly, he picked up his knife and cut his sandwich too. He didn't tend to dip his sandwiches, but if Hannah was doing it…

She bit her lower lip as she thought about the question. Watching her bite her lip had to be the sexiest thing he'd ever seen a woman do when she wasn't meaning to actually be sexy. His dick hardened in response, and he swallowed a groan, cursing at himself.

He was *not* gonna get a hard-on over his daughter's teacher thinking about teaching.

"I love helping others," she said quietly, her full lips pursed to blow on the hot soup.

*Is she trying to drive me insane?*

No, Hannah Lambert was just that innocent. She had an air about her that practically screamed her innocence from the rooftop.

"Ever since I was a child," she said after taking a sip of the soup, "I knew I'd be a teacher. It's what I was meant to be, you know? Michelle Winthrop – you know her? Works down at the pound as the city animal control officer?"

He nodded, listening and wondering where this was going. Of course he knew Michelle – she was also older than him, but she had the kind of forceful personality that meant she stood out in every crowd. She was on the larger side, which Elijah figured was a big help when she had to wrestle stray animals into submission.

He didn't want to come up against her in an arm wrestling contest, that was for damn sure.

"She's always loved animals," Hannah continued, "but she'd never planned on being the city animal control officer. Her first love is horses, and she'd wanted to race them, but...anyway, so she's still working with animals and she's a great advocate for them, but I think she could take it or leave it at the city."

Hannah let out a long sigh, like the weight of the world was on her shoulders.

"Me? This is all I want to do; all I'll ever do; and I'm happy there. Some classes are harder than others, and the paperwork end of things is only getting worse by the year. Some days, I spend more time filling out paperwork than I do actually teaching children, and that drives me crazy. The pay...don't even get me started on how pathetic teacher pay is, and on top of it all, I buy things for my classroom out of my own pocket all the time." Her jaw tightened up a little and he wondered if being poor made her life as miserable as it made his. "But," she finally said, shrugging, "teaching is my passion, so I take the lumps with it."

And with that, she went as quiet as a church mouse, the curtain dropping over her, blocking out the world, and him along with it. She dipped the last of her sandwich into her soup and popped it into her mouth, chewing and staring over his shoulder into the kitchen, not meeting his gaze.

He openly stared at her, trying to figure out what was going on in that gorgeous red head of hers. She'd been talking endlessly, and then…nothing. He figured that trying to drag words out of her when she was like this would be like trying to take a cat on a walk – it wasn't gonna work real well and they'd both be pissed off by the end.

But somehow, he felt compelled to take the damn cat on a walk.

"Why do you shut down on me sometimes?" he asked bluntly.

"Shut down?" she repeated, glancing at him so hurriedly, he didn't think she'd even met his gaze, and then her eyes were pinned on her soup, like it held the secret to eternal life or something.

"Yeah. You talk and I love listening to you, and then, all of the sudden, you're Fort Knox over there, not looking at me, not talking. You hide."

There was a part of Elijah that wished that he had Aaron's gift of gab. He could make this sound so much better than Elijah was doing. But if he was gonna have a relationship with Hannah of any kind, he couldn't keep having her shut him out every other sentence.

Not, of course, that he was gonna have a relationship with her. This was just a one-and-done date.

Nothing more.

She pushed at the bridge of her nose, coloring an adorable pink when she realized that she wasn't wearing her glasses. "I'm…I'm not hiding!" she protested hotly.

He stared at her, one eyebrow cocked, and he waited. He knew that she'd have to fill the silence, and he wanted to know what she'd fill it with.

Sure enough, after roughly an eternity and a half or so, she broke.

"People are scary," she said seriously, nibbling on her bottom lip with her cute, not-horse-sized teeth. "Well, adults are scary," she added. "Kids are not. But adult males are the worst of all. You men are downright terrifying, I hope you know that."

She said it with all of the seriousness of a doctor proclaiming that their patient was dying of cancer.

"You're shittin' me, right?" Elijah asked, stunned. "Guys make sense. It's girls who are scary."

She stood up from the table and began clearing away the dishes, carrying them into the kitchen without sparing him a glance. "I'm sure I don't know what you mean," she sniffed. "Women are perfectly logical creatures who don't impulsively say things like, 'Hold my beer!' and then jump off a cliff into an icy cold lake. You'd never catch a woman doing things like that. And anyway, women are kind, and mostly easy to talk to, whereas guys just—"

He snatched the washcloth out of her hands and gave her his best charming grin. He wasn't Aaron, so charming wasn't his strong suit, but he did his best.

Based on the heat rising in her cheeks, he felt pretty confident he'd succeeded.

"Whereas guys just wanna kiss you?" He finished her sentence for her, tossing the washcloth carelessly into the kitchen sink and then began backing her towards the counter, his hands burrowing into her thick, dark red hair. He'd never seen that particular shade of red outside of the hair salon, but he'd be willing to bet his right ball sac that it was natural. Made him wonder what color other hair on her was...

"Only...only this one guy," she whispered, her huge blue

eyes even more huge and blue than they'd ever been before. "And he only did it once, so…"

"That sounds like a challenge," he whispered, before he finally kissed that delicious mouth the way he'd wanted to for the last hour, ever since he'd come up for air after the last bout of kissing. She tasted so damn good. He tilted her head for easier access, wanting to devour her or melt into her or—

She broke him, then.

She made the tiniest of noises in the back of her throat, and she broke him. A million little pieces, right there on the floor.

He pulled away, his heart pounding, and he shook his head. "I better take you home," he said, his words slurred together from the heat burning between them.

If he'd ever felt like this while kissing Sarah, he damn well couldn't remember it. Surely he'd never felt this kind of fire roar through his veins before.

And that scared the shit right out of him. He didn't know if he *wanted* to be one-and-done with her.

And that scared him most of all.

# CHAPTER 20

## ELIJAH

ANOTHER WEEK, another dollar. Except today wasn't just another day at work. Today was when he had to go into Hannah's classroom and sweep and mop and empty her garbages and pretend like nothing – nothing at all – had happened over the weekend.

That they were just friends, and nothing more.

Because he'd had the past two days to think it all through, and to realize that he didn't deserve anything more than "just friends." She was smart. She spoke proper, she had a degree in teaching, and she knew more in her little pinky than he did in his whole body, about pert near everything.

Not only was she good at school, she even taught school. They'd never put him in charge of teaching anyone, unless it was on how to run a gas station at night, or how to mop floors, or how to knock up your girlfriend when you didn't mean to.

Like that was something the men of the world needed help with.

So yeah, she was roughly 937 pay grades or so above him, and he needed to leave her the hell alone so she could move on. Find someone as smart as her and they could have little nerdy adorable children together who wore thick coke-bottle glasses that distorted their eyes, but were somehow all the more cute for it.

With a deep breath, he pushed his way into her classroom and…

Just being in there – yeah, it was as bad as he thought it was gonna be. She looked up at him, confusion and hesitation and excitement written all over her face, and he knew that she didn't know why he'd dropped her off on her front doorstep on Friday night without saying a word and had driven off into the night.

And damn his dirty hide, he didn't have it in him to tell her.

He dropped his eyes and stared down at his cart. "Miss Lambert," he said formally, nodding in her general direction and pulling on the brim of his cap before going around the room to pick up the trash.

*Don't go looking at her. Then you'll just want her more and you can't have her. Shouldn't have had her before. Kissing her, listening to her make that little noise that you aren't ever gonna forget…that's what you get for trying with a woman like her – you get to hear that noise on repeat for the rest of your damn life.*

"Mr. Morland," Hannah said in return, except it came out as a question instead of all formal-like, like she'd wanted to sound, and he knew – just knew – that her big ol' blue eyes were tracking him as he went around the room, asking him questions he didn't have any answers for.

He swept the room in record time, kicking up more dust and dirt than he was sweeping up, and the burning red of his neck just got hotter as the tension in the room got thicker.

By time he was done sweeping, he figured he could cut that tension with his boning knife.

"Mr. Morland?" Hannah said questioningly, and this time, she didn't try to pretend that she wasn't confused as hell.

"You got something I can clean or fix for ya?" he tossed back curtly, refusing to look her in the eye as he dumped the little bit of dirt he managed to sweep up into the trashcan on his cart. It was a pathetic amount of dirt, honestly, and she'd have every right to complain to the principal about the job he'd just done, but he knew she wouldn't.

That wasn't Hannah's way.

"N-n-noo," she stuttered.

"Well then, you have a real nice day," and he left.

He was supposed to be mopping her floors now, but God knew, he'd have to sweep again before he could mop and he was dying, just dying, and he couldn't bear to be around her anymore, and he sure as hell couldn't sweep her room again, what with her staring at him with those big blue eyes the whole time.

No how, no way.

He hurried down the hallway and into the neighboring classroom and felt his chest tighten up as he went, but he ignored the pain.

He deserved what he got.

He'd never get anything more, and that was just how it should be.

# CHAPTER 21

## HANNAH

November, 2018

THE ARCTIC WIND whipped by but none of the kids seemed to notice, bundled up as they were against the frigid winter air. Hannah pulled her thick down jacket closer around her, trying to keep her teeth from chattering as she looked out over the playground, watching closely for any signs of trouble. Daisy was standing next to her, as usual, talking a mile a minute about her horse and training it to jump and Hannah listened with half an ear, making sure to make all of the right noises at all of the right times. Daisy was one of those children who latched onto a teacher rather than making friends with kids her own age, and thus, recess was spent talking the ear off whichever teacher had recess duty that week.

She was a cute kid, if a little overwhelming at times.

And then Hannah saw it – a group of kids in a circle, all facing inward towards someone she couldn't see, the whole thing setting off her teacher spidey senses, as she liked to think of them. There was something wrong there, she was sure of it, and she took off at a quick trot, telling Daisy that she'd be right back, zeroing in on the group and hoping to get there before they realized she was coming and had a chance to run.

Alas, it didn't work – it rarely did – but the kids scattering like leaves in the wind revealed Brooklyn standing there, sobbing her eyes out and blindly trying to hide her face from the rest of the world by burying it in the sleeve of her cute new jacket, much like an ostrich would hide from the world.

"Hey, Brooklyn," Hannah said softly, wrapping her arm around the girl's thin shoulders. "Are you okay? What's going on?"

The little girl shook her head violently, the tears streaming down her face, snuffling loud enough to be heard a block over. The tears on her cheeks in this cold…honestly, she'd be snuffling her nose whether she was crying or not.

Hannah looked up and caught the eye of the aide who had recess duty that week, and waved at her to let her know she was going into the building, and then quickly guided Brooklyn inside and down to her classroom. She closed the door behind them to give them privacy, before she turned and kneeled in front of Brooklyn. She wasn't particularly tall, but neither was Brooklyn, so this just about made them eye to eye.

"You need to tell me what's going on," she said softly to the distraught student in front of her, pushing the greasy-looking hair out of Brooklyn's face. Sarah may've started dressing her daughter better, but she sure hadn't begun washing her more often.

"Brooklyn needs a bath," she said in a mocking singsong voice, and then started blubbering, "That's what they was sayin'." The tears were creating light streaks through the dirt on her cheeks, and Hannah ground her back teeth together.

"When was the last time you took a bath or a shower, Brooklyn?" she asked quietly, running her hands up and down the frail shoulders consolingly.

"I don't like showers," she announced. "I don't like water in my face."

Hannah nodded understandingly, even as she noticed what Brooklyn wasn't telling her – the last time she'd had a bath.

And then she realized: She might not even know.

Hannah forced herself to focus on the here and now, even as she mentally wrapped her hands around Sarah's neck and strangled her.

"How about we do this?" she said gently. "Let's go down to the bathroom and scrub all of these…tears," she stumbled over the word, "off your face. You'll feel better after that, I promise."

*Not to mention the layer of dirt I'll be stripping off.*

Brooklyn shrugged but still, she slipped her hand trustingly into Hannah's as they walked down the hallway to the bathroom. Hannah's mind spun as she tried to work through her options.

Elijah cared but had very little home time with Brooklyn, plus there was the fact that Hannah would almost rather set herself on fire than talk to Eli. One magical evening where everything went so wonderfully wrong, and ever since, he'd been treating her like she had leprosy.

Then Sarah…Hannah had yet to meet the woman, despite having held two nights of parent-teacher conferences thus far in the school year.

To put it politely, the mother didn't seem to have much in the way of interest in her daughter's education.

To put the nicest spin possible on the situation.

As Hannah knelt in front of Brooklyn and scrubbed her elfin face with a damp paper towel, she tried to figure out some way to help. The neglect wasn't bad enough to call Child Protective Services on Sarah – if she called CPS every time a child was sent to school with a dirty face and greasy hair, she'd be doing nothing but that for the rest of the school year.

There was a giant gap between what CPS cared about, and what the kids on the playground cared about, though, and Hannah wasn't sure what to do in that in-between spot.

Finally, Brooklyn's face was clean and shining, but her hair…yup, dirty blonde was a pretty apt description of it.

Then inspiration struck and she quickly checked her watch.

"We have four minutes left until the bell rings," she told Brooklyn. "Let's hurry back to the classroom. I think I know just what to do."

Hand in hand, they hurried back down the hallway to Hannah's classroom and over to her desk. Pulling the bottom drawer open, Hannah pulled out some sparkling bows and then from her middle drawer, she pulled out her own hairbrush.

At the sight of the hair clips, Brooklyn's eyes went wide and she squealed with delight, that particular high-pitched noise only ten-year-old girls can make. "So pretty, Miss Lambert!" she exclaimed.

Hannah had paid for them out of her own pocket to use as prizes in the classroom reading program, knowing that the girls would go spastic over them, but hey, if there was ever a little girl who needed a pretty hair barrette, it was Brooklyn.

"You get it off the packaging while I brush your hair. We'll have you done up in no time. We gotta hurry – the bell's about to ring."

As Brooklyn tore into the packaging, Hannah hurriedly ran the brush through her blonde hair, trying to get the snarls out without tugging too hard. Considering the state of it, though, she should add detangler to her shopping list the next time she went to Boise.

With all of that spare money she had sitting around in her bank account, of course.

Ignoring that reality for the moment, she focused on what needed to happen: Step Two in her plan.

"Brooklyn," she announced as she pulled the hairbrush through the little girl's greasy hair, "I'm gonna call your mom after school." Brooklyn froze, standing in front of her, facing away into the classroom so Hannah couldn't see her face, but she could tell that Brooklyn thought this was a good plan, just like she'd think that being stuck with Dayton as her partner for the rest of the year would be a good plan. "Tomorrow is the beginning of Thanksgiving break, so I'm going to tell her that starting on Monday, she needs to bring you in before school each day so I can tutor you in math."

Ignoring Hannah's attempts to clip the barrette into place, Brooklyn turned around and glared at her teacher suspiciously. "I'm doing real good in math!" she protested. "I got a B+ on the last math test, and—"

The bell rang, and Hannah spoke quickly before the rest of the class could arrive. "You come before school starts, and I'll help you get ready every morning. Wash your hair, brush your teeth – all of it. No more 'Brooklyn needs a bath' at recess."

"Really?!" Brooklyn squealed, all anger and suspicion instantly gone. "Thank you, Miss Lambert!" She threw her arms around Hannah's waist and hugged her as hard as she could with her thin little arms.

Hannah hugged her back, mentally going over everything she'd need to buy out of her meager teacher salary to make this happen.

Being a teacher was mentally and emotionally rewarding, but financially…not so much. She had to stop doing this sort of thing, but seeing a need and not helping…she might as well quit being a teacher.

Her mind flashed over to ~~Elijah~~ Mr. Morland. What would he have to say about this?

It only took a hot second to decide – she wouldn't tell him, any more than she was going to tell Ms. Morland the truth. What mattered was the well being of her student, and if she had to be a little sneaky to make it happen, well then, that's what she'd do.

# CHAPTER 22

## ELIJAH

"THEY'RE PINK, my favorite color!" Brooksy told him as she held his hand, standing in the lunch line, waiting ever so impatiently to get through the line to sit at one of the too-small-for-him tables to eat lunch.

Elijah looked down at her and nodded absentmindedly. "Did your mom buy them for you when she took you school clothes shopping?" he asked, at least happy to imagine that his hard-earned money had paid for something that made his daughter happy, especially since he didn't have much more where that came from.

Even as he spoke, his mind was going 'round and 'round, worry eating away at him. It was December, which meant he should be coming up with a Christmas present or two for Brooksy, but his power bill was outta control this month…the whole thing made his stomach clench with panic. He'd been meaning to put an ad in the newspaper about handyman work to bring in some extra income, but life had gotten away from—

"Noooo…" Brooksy drew the word out, and then it was their turn to pick up a tray each and begin working their way down the line. He had to wait to question her 'cause the cafeteria ladies were all laughing and flirting with him, even the ones old enough to be his grandmother, as they dished out the food. They'd told him a long time ago that he could eat there for free, since he did "such a good job" cleaning the cafeteria after lunch each day.

It was a child-sized meal so it didn't fill him up entirely, but he wasn't about to complain. Free food was free food.

He waited until they were out of earshot of the overly flirtatious cafeteria workers and were sliding onto the benches at their favorite way-too-small table, before he begun pushing Brooksy for answers. "What do you mean, 'no'?" he asked her, his eyes flitting over the sparkly-and-ever-so-pink barrettes in his daughter's hair. They were the most girly barrettes that he ever did lay eyes on, so of course, Brooksy would love 'em.

Brooksy hesitated, chewing her bottom lip which was a sure sign something was wrong, and then Juniper and Juan slid in next to them and they began chatting about who could make the best horsey neigh, Elijah fell silent, letting Brooksy just be a kid for a minute.

It was weird enough that he worked at her school and ate lunch with her every day and walked her over to the school bus line every afternoon. He didn't need to keep her from just being her while around her friends, too.

He hurriedly ate the last of his applesauce before they put their lunch trays away in the large gray tubs and Brooksy began tugging him to drag him outside. "I gotta go do something," she told her friends. "I'll be right back." The two kids shrugged and ran off towards the swing set while Brooksy dragged him towards the 5th grade building…and straight into Hannah's classroom.

*Shiiittttt. Of course.*

His stomach clenched up again, just like it had while he'd been thinking about paying for his power bill and Christmas at the same time, but this time, he couldn't just swallow the panic down because there was Hannah, at her desk, eating a sandwich with one hand while grading papers with the other.

His eyes ate her up hungrily. She'd curled her hair and had put in her contacts that day, but as far as he could tell, she wasn't wearing a bit of makeup. She was damn pretty even without the makeup, and he wanted to run his fingers through her hair to see if he was rightly remembering how soft it was, or if he was making it up.

*No* woman's hair was that soft.

The palms of his hands itched to touch it, begging him to settle the matter once and for all.

Hannah looked up absentmindedly from the papers when she heard them come in, and then shot to her feet, sending a frantic smile at him and Brooksy, plopping her half-eaten sandwich down on top of the pile of papers she'd been working on. "Hi, Brooklyn," she said, focusing those beautiful blue eyes on his daughter. "You brought your dad in to talk to me?" He couldn't help but notice she wasn't making eye contact with him. Nope, Hannah was staring straight at his daughter and nowhere else.

Brooksy shook her head, her Pepto Bismol pink barrette sparkling in the light. "Nope. I wanna show him my drawer." She tugged him over so that he was practically standing shoulder to shoulder with Hannah as Brooksy proudly pulled a drawer open in her teacher's desk.

*Why are we looking in Hannah's desk? My daughter shouldn't just be going 'round and opening up drawers without permission from—*

"She's got it all in here," Brooksy said with a huge grin up at him. Confused as hell, he looked past his daughter's delighted face and into the drawer itself. It was filled to the brim with every item a soul could need to get ready in the morning, and then some. Toothbrush, toothpaste, floss, face wipes, hairbrush, leave-in conditioner, even shampoo, and then a bunch of colorful hair ties and shit.

*What the hell? Is Hannah running herself a beauty parlor outta her classroom? What is this?*

As his mind spun, trying to figure out what in the good Lord his daughter was showing him, she kept talking. "Momma brings me to school early," Brooksy explained, "and Miss Lambert takes me down to the bathroom and helps me wash my hair in the sink when it needs it, and then I brush my teeth and stuff." She stopped for a moment and then added, "No one's called me Stinky Brooksy in a long time, neither."

Elijah scrambled to put the pieces together. Kids had been calling his daughter Stinky Brooksy?! Since when? And why wasn't Sarah doing this stuff at home with Brooksy? He'd thought his daughter had been looking a little on the crummy side there for a while, but then she started looking good again, and he didn't think any more about it.

That was Hannah's doing? He looked up at Hannah to find a funny look on her face, and he knew that she was worried about him taking it all wrong. And it *was* hard for him to see it 'cause this was his daughter and his family wasn't a charity case, needing to be taken care of by someone else, no damn way.

But at the same time, she was doing something that really needed to be done since his ex wasn't, and for that, he was eternally grateful.

Brooksy was staring up at him expectantly, waiting for him to say something, so he pushed the words out. "And your momma brings you to school early for this?" That, more than anything else, surprised the hell outta him. Sarah wasn't what he'd call an early riser.

Hannah helping his daughter? She was the nicest woman he'd ever met, so that didn't surprise him at all.

But Sarah never did anything she didn't have to.

"Well, to study math." Brooksy shot a grin up at him, waiting for him to catch up to what she was saying. "But my math is real good, so instead, we just clean me up."

Of course. It all made sense, then.

Grades were tangible – something he could point to in court to prove Sarah wasn't doing a good job of raising Brooksy. His daughter'd always done well in school – thank God she got something good from her momma – so if her grades fell off a cliff, Sarah would know Eli could use that against her in the courtroom. If Hannah had told Sarah that Brooksy needed extra studying time in the mornings, well, it was probably the only thing that could motivate Sarah to get her ass outta bed before noon – beating Elijah in court.

"You…you been doing this for a while?" he asked, past the lump in his throat.

He wasn't sure if he was thrilled to have Hannah as his daughter's teacher, or pissed as hell to have Sarah as his ex-wife.

Both, really.

"Just a couple of weeks," Brooksy said. Hannah still hadn't said a word, and Elijah wondered what she was thinking. "I can't tell Momma because she'd get real mad, but I thought it was okay to tell you because you won't tell Momma. Right?"

"No, I won't tell her," he promised his suddenly anxious daughter. She settled right down and shot him a huge grin.

"I knew you wouldn't," she said proudly. Just then, the lunch bell rang and almost instantly, the hallways filled with the buzzing sound of swarming children.

"I best get back to work." He tugged the brim of his ball cap towards Hannah and then gave Brooksy a quick hug goodbye. "See you after school," he promised his daughter, and quickly headed out of the brightly decorated classroom and down to his closet to get out the cleaning supplies for his afternoon jobs.

Maybe he'd do a deep cleaning of the boy's bathroom and think about life for a while and what to do about certain teachers named Hannah.

He sure needed to come up with something because as it was, he just had no clue.

# CHAPTER 23

## HANNAH

"DON'T FORGET to work on your autobiography this evening," Hannah called out over the ringing of the final bell. "Your rough drafts are due tomorrow."

The kids weren't paying a bit of attention to her as they busily stuffed their backpacks and laughed and chatted, thrilled that school was finally over.

For once, Hannah was grateful they were tuning her out.

She sank down in her wobbly chair behind her desk and stared out blankly into the emptying classroom, unsure of what to think or say or do. Brooklyn's arrival at lunchtime, tugging the hand of her father along to show him "her drawer" had surprised the heck out of her, and thinking back on what she'd taught after that, she had a hard time remembering any of it.

Had she even taught anything at all? She was sure she had, but it was all just a blur now.

It really wasn't fair that a man who didn't seem to think she was worth even the slightest bit of effort to tell her what she'd done that was so darn awful, was also the same man who set her whole body on fire. She remembered back to Mr. Kiener, asking her out for coffee before school started. She could've had a hundred Mr. Kieners march into her classroom to talk to her, and it wouldn't have affected her one teensy-weensy little bit.

But oh no, just one Mr. Elijah Morland, and her body went simply nuts.

*Gah.* She groaned as she looked up at the clock, biting her lower lip. She had 40 minutes until Elijah would be in her classroom again, cleaning it like he did every afternoon.

What was she going to say? Finally confront him about what had been the world's best date that had ended in the world's worst way? Talk to him about when she'd called Sarah to discuss tutoring her daughter in math before school, Sarah's words had been slurred to the point that Hannah wasn't sure how much of the conversation the woman would remember afterwards? Tell him that he had the most darling daughter she'd ever had the good fortune to teach? Ask him what it was about her that was so repugnant that just the idea of talking to her sent him running in the other direction?

Well, she had – she looked up at the clock again – 37 minutes to figure it out.

It would help if she'd been able to tell if he was pissed or happy or angry or thrilled that she'd been helping clean Brooklyn up before school each day. As his daughter had been talking, his face…

Inscrutable.

Every time she thought she knew him, he'd change on her all over again. She considered herself to be a fairly intelligent person, but Elijah confounded her in ways that no textbook could solve. On the one hand, she knew he had more pride than a whole group of lions, so seeing what someone outside of the family was doing for his daughter was probably a punch to the gut.

But on the other hand, he had one place where he was willing to sacrifice all pride – his daughter. No doubt becoming a janitor at her school wasn't an easy decision to make, but he'd been willing to do it because of Brooklyn.

So, was he pissed or happy or angry or thrilled about her cleaning Brooklyn up every day?

She dropped her forehead onto her desk with a thunk, and then snuck a peek up at the clock on the wall. She had 29—

She saw movement out of the corner of her eye, and turned her head slightly to see Elijah in the doorway.

She had exactly no minutes left to figure out what she was going to say.

If she was a swearing woman, she'd be letting a blue streak loose right about now. She unhappily settled on a plastered-on smile instead.

"Mr. Morland," she said formally, rising to her feet as if she hadn't just been slumped over with her head on the desk. Ignoring reality – it was one of her best talents. She forced herself to walk to the side of her desk and not use the large wooden surface as a barrier between them. If she was being truly brave, she'd stand in front of her desk or even – God forbid – walk over to him, but…

Apparently, her big girl panties were only partially on today – caught, perhaps, somewhere around her kneecaps.

Which might explain why she had such a hard time walking. It had to be that.

He pushed his cleaning cart inside of her classroom but then abandoned it – and any pretense of cleaning – by the open doorway.

"I've…I've been thinking about it all afternoon," he said as he came – ever so slowly – closer to her, shuffling his feet like an errant schoolboy as he went. "I don't know how to feel 'bout having someone else taking care of my daughter like that, but since I only got her for two days every other weekend, I don't know how to fix it myself, and…" He rubbed the back of his neck which was growing brighter red by the moment, as he stared down at the floor. "I shoulda noticed before now. She had all of those new clothes that she was always showing off, and I guess I didn't look any further than that."

He was standing close enough to touch by now, and without thinking, Hannah did exactly that. She put her hand out and laid it on his arm to console him, except…

His mesmerizing gray-green eyes flicked up to hers, dark with lust.

*No, no, that isn't right.*

She had to be reading him wrong, because it had only taken him one date to realize that she was the least sexy woman to ever walk the planet. How many other guys kissed a girl twice, and then pretended that they were escapees from a leprosy colony? As far as Hannah had been able to figure out over the past two months, she must be the least desirable woman Elijah had ever had the misfortune to kiss.

So why was he looking at her like he wanted to eat her up with a spoon?

And then, just like the night of botched trips to pizza parlors and burnt deer steaks and her blubbering up a storm on his shirt about her father, he was burying his hands in her hair and pulling her towards him and kissing her as if his very life depended on it.

Her knees were going weak and, like the heroines in the cheesy romance novels she used to sneak into her bedroom when she was a teenager, she felt herself clinging to him with all her might, telling herself to be practical and keep her feet underneath her, but deep down in her soul, she was wanting to just be swept away to a world where things weren't complicated and dating him wasn't forbidden and mothers actually loved their children and—

She stiffened a bit, just a half second before Elijah did. Her eyes flew open and she yanked away from him and spun towards the classroom door, smoothing her hands over the front of her slacks as her aide, Amelia, shot her a naughty grin.

"I'm just here to grab my purse," Amelia said airily, sauntering over to her small desk shoved in the corner, covered with all of the projects Hannah kept her busy with. "Don't let me interrupt."

Hannah could see Elijah doing something out of the corner of her eye, but she was too embarrassed to look over to see exactly what it was. As for her, her hands had moved from smoothing her slacks to smoothing her hair. The way Elijah had been cradling her head in his calloused hands, she probably looked like she'd been thoroughly kissed.

Which was exactly what had been happening, of course. Was it possible to die of mortification? She was pretty sure it was. She cursed the fair skin that came along with her red hair and blue eyes. She had roughly a 0.00% chance of hiding the blush stealing over her entire body in that moment.

She felt Elijah's fingers on her chin, and she turned to look up at him. Instead of looking embarrassed as heck over getting caught necking like teenagers in the broom closet, he looked like the cat that'd caught the canary. "I better finish my rounds," he said with a lustful grin, "but why don't I come over to your place around five, and we can finish our...discussion then."

She nodded weakly, and then sank into her chair as Elijah left the room, whistling innocently as he went, pulling on the brim of his ball cap as he passed Amelia. "Good afternoon," he said to Hannah's aide, as formally as if they were in a drawing room sipping tea, and then with a clatter of stuff, he was off to the next classroom to clean.

Amelia shot an amazed look over her shoulder at the empty doorway and then at Hannah.

"How long have you two been dating?!" she practically whisper-shouted as she dashed over to Hannah's desk to stare down at her in disbelief. "And how could you hide that from me?!"

"I'm not sure we are dating," Hannah said truthfully. "The last time he kissed me like that, he didn't speak to me for two months."

Two months and six days, to be precise, not that she'd been counting or anything.

"The last time?" Amelia asked, her jaw practically scraping on the ground. "Hannah Lambert, I didn't know you had it in you!"

"What, to kiss a handsome guy?" Hannah retorted dryly. She knew she wasn't the most experienced of women, but surely *kissing* seemed like something she'd do.

"Kiss the father of a student and a guy who also happens to be your coworker! Does the principal know about this?"

"Of course not!" Hannah said, horrified at the idea. "Dear Lord above, no. It only happened one other time and then… nothing. For months. So I didn't think he liked me."

"Oh, he likes you," Amelia said, and started howling with laughter. "I promise you, he likes you!"

Hannah glared at her aide, who she'd always loved and adored up to that point. That feeling was quickly beginning to fade, though, with every howl of laughter.

Amelia caught the look in Hannah's eye and held up her hands defensively. "Sorry, I shouldn't laugh," she said, completely unrepentant, the corners of her mouth struggling to stay in a level line. Hannah rolled her eyes at her aide's transparent insincerity. "So, are you leaving?"

"Leaving?" Hannah asked, completely confused by the change in topic. "Oh, changing schools, you mean?"

It was something she'd thought about doing, although she hated to leave Cleveland Elementary. It was the only school she'd ever taught at, and she was comfortable here. The idea of meeting a whole new roster of adults made her break out into a cold sweat. But it would solve all of their problems, even if she wouldn't be able to do it until the end of the school year. And then there was the fact that she'd be commuting to Franklin each day as a best-case scenario, if not Boise, and how would that affect her checking in on her dad and her horses, and—

"Going home," Amelia said bluntly. *Oh, right, of course.* "And getting ready for Mr. Morland," she waggled her eyebrows as she said his name, "to come over to…discuss things with you."

The way she said it, Hannah knew Amelia didn't think they'd be doing much talking at all, and the thing was, she wasn't sure if she wanted Amelia to be wrong or not.

This was all easy enough for Amelia to suggest; it wasn't her who'd look like an idiot if it all fell apart again. The logical side of her wanted to tell Amelia that of course she wasn't going to go home to get ready to see Elijah. She was going to stay right there at her desk and get all of the things done that always needed to be done, and she wasn't going to be tempted by his ever-changing eyes, or the way his front teeth overlapped just a smidge, or his sleek muscles that she wanted to—

She groaned again.

"What if I get all gussied up," she whispered, "but he's really coming over to tell me that he doesn't want to kiss me anymore?" She was only willing to say the nightmare scenario out loud because she was discussing the topic with Amelia. If it'd been any other teacher, she never, ever would've had the guts to say it. "I'll look like an idiot, expecting something that he's not actually wanting to give."

Amelia opened her mouth to tell Hannah that she was a few bricks shy of a full load, Hannah was just sure of it, when she paused and thought a while instead.

Finally, she said slowly, "Normally, I'd say you're talking crazy for saying something like that – that Elijah Morland has the hots for you, and there's no way he'd just walk away – but he did do this once before, sooo…"

She tapped her front teeth with her fingernail, her brow creased as she thought it all through. As Hannah watched and waited, she realized that she wasn't even sure if she knew what she was hoping her aide would tell her, only that she needed to have someone else's take on the situation because she just went around and around and around in her head when she tried to puzzle it all out.

"I get the worry," Amelia said after a long silence, looking her straight in the eye. "Truly, I do – I'm not just saying that. But Hannah, you've got to be willing to give it a try. If you always expect the men in the world to disappoint you, you're always going to be disappointed. Damn, girl, this is a guy who's willing to walk across broken glass for his daughter; any woman he loves, he'll love her just as deeply. And yeah, maybe he's not in love with you yet, but after seeing you two kiss…I promise you, he's quickly getting there." She picked Hannah's purse up from the floor and shoved it into her hands. "Now, go get yourself gussied up. He's gonna be worth it, I promise."

Hannah swallowed hard, a ball of panic roiling around in her stomach, and then nodded. Clutching her purse against her chest, she dashed for the classroom door.

She had until five o'clock to make herself look so good, Elijah could never bear to walk away.

Only 96 minutes to make a miracle happen.

# CHAPTER 24

## ELIJAH

CLUTCHING THE COLORING PAD to his chest, Elijah cursed his stupidity under his breath. Boy howdy, he'd done some awfully stupid things in his time, but honestly, who gave a coloring book to a woman as a present? What were they – ten?

Sure, Hannah liked to color, and sure, she liked to put the finished pictures up all over her classroom which he'd admired plenty of times, but still, shouldn't he be bringing her chocolates or some more flowers?

It was Carla who'd told him no. "You bought her purple-and-white daisies already," she'd told him when he'd stopped by Happy Petals for another bouquet. "You're not going to be able to top that. You can't do better than her all-time favorite flowers, right? So, pick something else. What else does Hannah absolutely love?"

"Children, her horses, and her father," Elijah had said, rattling them off without batting an eyelash.

Carla had stared at him for a moment.

"Huh. Well, that's true," she'd allowed, "but since you can't give her children – at least, I hope you're not planning on that right now – and she sure doesn't need another horse or another father, what else can you give her that she enjoys doing to relax?"

"Coloring!" he'd exclaimed, like he'd just figured out how to solve world hunger.

"Oh, perfect!" she'd praised him. "There are some fun coloring books over in Franklin. You should go on down to Once Upon a Trinket and check them out."

*Huh.* It wasn't until just now, remembering back on how all that went down, that he realized Carla may've known that answer from the get-go, and had just been leading him along, trying to get him to come up with the idea all on his own so he could feel like he'd really accomplished something special.

*Damn, she's good…*

*Sneaky as hell, but good.*

He realized with a start that he was about to strangle the coloring book into a big wad o' shit, and forced himself to stop trying to roll it up like a paper towel tube.

*Breathe. You're gonna be fine. She was kissing you real nice earlier today, so she isn't gonna slam the door in your face now—*

"That's it, I can't stand it anymore," Hannah announced, yanking the door open just as he raised his hand to knock.

Elijah's mouth gaped open as he stared at her. He had no idea she could be so forceful. Or that she'd been standing on the other side of the door, watching him debate whether he was messing this all up.

"Well, are you just going to hang around on my front porch like you have nothing else to do, or are you coming in?" she demanded, her hands on her slim hips.

He couldn't help the huge smile that spread over his face. He may not know who this Hannah Lambert was, but he was liking her anyway.

"Coming in right now," he said smartly as he sidled past her and into the warmth of her family's home. "I…uh…brought a present for you." He held the coloring book out to her, hoping she didn't notice that it was all curled up on the edges.

Her eyes lit up and she sent him a huge smile as she reached for it, their fingertips brushing for just a split second as she took it from him.

"I can't believe you," she murmured, all sweet and quiet again. She thumbed through the pages of central Idaho drawings, ready to be brought to life. He'd bought it 'cause it was a coloring book done up by a local gal by the name of Ivy Bishop – she used to be a McLain. She'd graduated three years ahead of him in school but even back then, everyone had known she was real good with a pencil and paintbrush and now she was using that talent to make the prettiest drawings he'd ever seen.

"I'm…I'm sorry about that," Hannah murmured, her cheeks turning red as she jerked her head towards the front door, keeping her eyes glued on the drawings in the book. "I don't normally spy on people who are standing on my front porch, I promise."

"Yeah, well, I don't normally stand on a front porch for ten minutes, either," he mumbled, feeling his own face turn red. She probably thought he was one dumb idiot for that stunt but honestly, that's 'cause he *was* an idiot when it came to Hannah Lambert.

Maybe Aaron was good at schmoozing the ladies, but whatever talent he got from their parents, Elijah didn't have one little bit of it.

Apparently, all of the courage that she'd screwed up in order to confront him on the front porch had disappeared, 'cause she'd set the coloring book down and was back to twisting her hands together, looking him over awkwardly as he did the same to her.

It wasn't until then that he realized what an amazing top she had on.

Amazing, as in sexy as hell.

*Wowee!*

He'd known she had a nice set of tits on her, but it'd always been a theoretical knowledge, much like he knew that his parents had sex on a regular basis. That didn't mean that he'd ever seen it firsthand.

Unlike his parents having sex, though, he most definitely wanted to see proof of Hannah's tits.

"You…uhhh…look good. Real nice."

If he swallowed his own tongue, he couldn't be less suave than he was just then.

At his pathetic excuse of a compliment, her smile got all weird and he could read her clear as day – she wanted to know where things stood between them.

*You and me both.*

He took a deep breath. "Hannah, I like you," he said bluntly. "I'm not one to beat around the bush, so I'll just ask you straight out – will you be my girlfriend?"

She let out the tiniest of gasps and then said, "I would love to," all prim and proper-like, but her eyes – big and blue and gorgeous – were lit up like the 4th of July fireworks.

She liked him – she really liked him. She wasn't any good at hiding her feelings, thank God, and her thoughts were written clear as day all over her face.

The knot of worry and fear in his chest relaxed, and he realized with a start that he could breathe a little easier.

The silence between them, though, stretched out as they stared at each other. "Ummm…I don't rightly know what to do now," he finally admitted. "I haven't done this before."

She let out a little laugh – a giggle, really – that made him feel a whole lot better just for hearing it. He could listen to that sound all day long. "I haven't done this before, either. I haven't had…I haven't had a lot of boyfriends in my life." A dark cloud passed over her face as she said it, making him wonder if she had secrets that she wasn't sharing, at least not yet.

Well, that was okay. He had secrets, too. Everyone did, he figured.

"With Brooksy and Sarah and all, I think we oughta take it

slow. Between us. Like, we shouldn't go jumping into bed together or something."

He bumbled to a stop then because honestly, it wasn't possible to shove his booted foot any deeper down his throat – what on God's green earth made him bring up sex with her?! – but Hannah was just nodding along seriously. She should probably be slapping him but she wasn't, and wasn't that just lucky.

"I agree," she told him. "With my dad, and then being Brooklyn's teacher and of course, you're my coworker...I think the slower, the better."

"So, girlfriend," he said, testing the title out on his tongue and finding that he was liking it a whole lot, "you wanna color in your new book with me? I can't promise I'm any good, but..." He trailed off, shrugging.

"You'd color in a coloring book with me?" she asked, shocked as hell at the suggestion.

"Sure, why not," he said. "I've done plenty of coloring with Brooksy, so I'm not totally outta practice." And, as he figured it, if they were gonna move slow, there wasn't anything slower than coloring together. That was just one tiny step up from them both taking a vow of chastity and entering a monastery by the end of the night.

She shot him an excited grin. "Let me go get my coloring pencils. I'll be right back."

She hurried out of the room and down the hallway, leaving Elijah by himself to look around. He probably shouldn't be spying on her but...well, she did leave him in the room by himself. A look at the pictures on the wall wouldn't be prying, right?

It wasn't a real big house, but she was a good housekeeper and kept it nice. There was a gas fireplace with flames a-dancin' in it, and big bookshelves lining two of the walls. Lots of pictures of Hannah as a little girl were everywhere, some with her mom and dad, but most were just her by herself.

They all looked real happy together, and Elijah's heart ached a little.

First, she'd lost her mom to cancer when she was just little, if he remembered right, and now she'd all but lost her dad to dementia. Hell, he might as well be gone.

Elijah stopped in front of her high school graduation picture, proudly holding a sparkly "2002" on her lap for the year she'd graduated. Her small, cute little teeth; her dark red hair; her big blue eyes – they were all the same.

He stopped, something niggling at the back of his mind. There was something different here – something wrong. He looked over the picture again real carefully, but the school colors, the tassel, that stupid hat they were all forced to wear… just like it was supposed to be. He scanned her face again, and then it hit him – what *wasn't* there. Those damn thick glasses she used to wear – she wasn't wearing 'em here.

He heard her soft footsteps coming down the hallway and called out, "When did you start wearing those thick glasses?"

"What?!"

He looked over his shoulder at her, a little bit confused as to why she sounded like he'd just propositioned her momma. "Those glasses you were wearing at the beginning of the school year. In your high school graduation picture, you aren't wearing any glasses. I was just wondering when you started needing them."

She was as stiff as a piece of plywood. "I don't see why that is any of your business," she said flatly.

He pulled back, feeling like he'd just done a dance on razor-thin ice, but not knowing why. He held his hands up. "I was just wondering, is all. I didn't mean no harm."

She nodded just once and then said stiffly, "I wore contacts when I was in high school. I've needed corrective lenses since I was in second grade."

Elijah nodded, still not understanding why she was so pissed, but wanting to move onto something else before she got all bristly on him again. He pointed at another picture, this one of the garage only half built, her dad with a big ol' grin on his face and little Hannah next to him, red hair in braids, holding a hammer about as big as she was. "You helping your dad here?"

Her whole body relaxed just a little and she smiled sadly. "My dad wanted a real garage more than anything. My parents weren't wealthy, of course, and had to work hard and scrimp on everything to pay the mortgage off for this house. But my dad… he wanted a garage where he could work and stay out of the wind and rain and snow…he could do anything with his hands. I used to think he could build me a castle if I'd just asked, and I was probably right. He had this tiny cramped shed where he'd set up a project but he was always cursing the leaking roof and the lack of space…Finally building the garage was a dream come true for him."

"Pulling up here, I honestly didn't know that it was an addition to the house," Elijah told her seriously. "He did a real good job of matching the roofline and siding and such."

"He was a perfectionist, through and through."

Elijah couldn't help but notice that she was referring to her dad in the past tense, like he'd already up and died on her. In all of the important ways, Elijah guessed he had.

"So, you have the house now?" he asked, not sure if he was prying where he wasn't wanted, but curious anyhow.

"Mom died when I was only six, Dad's in the nursing home up on the hill, and I'm an only child, so…yeah, it's mine now. Paid off in full, so I only have to pay the taxes every year." She sent him a painful smile. "Honestly, I couldn't be a teacher otherwise. Teachers make so little money and are expected to buy supplies for their classroom on top of it…there's no other profession out there that asks so much and gives so little. And then people wonder why there's a teacher shortage." Hannah laughed bitterly. "I love my job, I do." She turned her huge blue eyes up at him, begging him to understand. "I hate to whine and complain, because it's my dream job and I'm lucky enough to be living it. I just wish that society appreciated us teachers more, and not just in 'I'm going to have my child bring an apple to school' way, but in real, honest-to-God ways that let us teachers not only teach children, but thrive as human beings."

And then, just like before, the curtain dropped and Hannah disappeared from view.

Oh, she was still standing right in front of him, but she might as well not have been. And then she was murmuring something under her breath as she hurried over to a huge wooden table with her coloring pencils in hand, the table all carved and fancy, and pulled two chairs out for them to sit in. She wasn't meeting his eye but instead was staring at the floor 'bout a foot in front of him like it was the most fascinating piece of carpet she'd ever seen.

"Hannah Lambert," he said harshly as he strode over to stand in front of her. Startled by his tone, her deep blue eyes rose to meet his. "You're doing it again. Talking and everything is great and then…bam! You're gone. Shush right up like you've sworn to never talk again. Why?" he demanded.

This time, he wasn't gonna let her sidetrack him. He was gonna get an answer outta her if it took all night.

Her pale cheeks went bright red and her golden lashes started fluttering up a storm as she looked this way and that, not meeting his gaze as she – transparent as a clean sheet of glass – tried to think of some good lie to tell him.

"You said months ago that fifth graders aren't good at lying," Elijah said bluntly. "Well, I'm thinking fifth grade teachers aren't any good either. I can see it all over your face – you're trying to think of a story to tell me. I suggest picking a real one."

That did it. Like letting off a swarm of bees up her skirt, Hannah got royally pissed. "How *dare* you say I was going to lie to you! What, are you a mind reader now? You can't—"

"I don't have to read minds to know what you're thinking," he interrupted her. "Your face says it all. You get this little dip right here," he traced a calloused finger between her eyebrows, "when you're thinking of a lie to tell."

She glared at him with everything in her body; hell, her toenails were probably glaring at him right then. "I don't tell lies. Ever. So you can just stop saying that this instant. As for shutting down, well, it's just that I realize that I'm talking way too much and I have to be boring you to death so it's best if I shut my mouth and stop putting you to sleep. Nobody wants to hear me talk about my father's obsession with a garage, for heaven's sakes. Or how teachers need to be paid what they're worth. They were ridiculous things to talk about and I don't know why I was saying those things to you." She drew in a deep breath, and then continued on, real quiet this time. "I say a lot of things to you that I don't say to other people and that scares me because…I shouldn't."

He cupped her cheek in the palm of his hand and turned her face to look up at him. "Why not?" he whispered, matching her volume. "I wanna hear every thought you have in your head. You're the most interesting person I've ever met. I wanna hear it all."

"You're just saying that to be kind," she protested, looking back down at the floor. "I'm not that interesting, I promise. I—"

"Well, I promise you are. So, what're you gonna say to that?" he challenged her. "It's up to me to say whether you're interesting to me or not, and I say you are. Are you calling me a liar?"

"Of course not!" she said, shocked. "I…well…I just…"

She stumbled to a stop, not real sure of where to go from there.

"Shy folks think that they don't have anything to say that's worth hearing. Well, the truth of the matter is, I do wanna hear it all. So, the next time that little voice in your head starts telling you some bullshit 'bout how I don't care, I want you to tell it to shut the hell up. Now, let's get to coloring and while we do, I want you to tell me every boring story you can think of 'bout your parents. I wanna hear them all."

He pulled a chair out for her and then sat in the other one, dumping out the colored pencils on the table for them to grab, and picked a simple forest scene to work on while, ever so slowly, Hannah began telling him funny stories and sad stories and thought-provoking stories and...

As she talked, she nibbled her lower lip thoughtfully, adding shading to the shadows of the pine trees and Elijah listened to it all, enjoying every minute but also wondering just how slow was slow.

If she kept nibbling her lower lip like that, he wasn't gonna be able to take it slow much longer.

He shifted in his seat and told himself to behave.

He just wasn't gonna look at her mouth ever again.

# CHAPTER 25

## HANNAH

"So then Juan raced across the finish line so far ahead of Dayton and Patrick," Brooklyn said excitedly, the chocolate chip cookie dough forgotten in her hands for the moment as she recounted the story, "heck, they probably couldn't even *see* him when he won," she boasted. "The PE teacher said that that was the fastest anyone had ever run the 500-meter in her class, and so of course Dayton and Patrick pretended like they weren't even trying to beat him but of course they were. I don't know why they think it's so bad to be Mexican."

Hannah squished her rounded ball of dough down onto the greased baking sheet as a subtle reminder to Brooklyn to do likewise, but Brooklyn being Brooklyn, of course the diversionary tactic didn't work. She kept her eyes pinned on Hannah while she dropped the ball of dough into place, the implied question hanging in the air.

Hannah squirmed a little inside, wishing that it was Elijah fielding this question. Racism was always a dicey topic, and then there was the fact that Hannah wasn't actually

Brooklyn's mother, even though she felt like she was most days, and…

She glanced up to find that yup, Brooklyn was still staring at her, her gray-green eyes glued to her every movement. Elijah had run down to the Shop 'N Go to get milk to dunk the cookies in, so for the moment, Hannah was it. They'd spent their Sunday together, the three of them, making cookies and playing Clue Jr. and even coloring some out of the gorgeous coloring book Elijah had given her over two months ago, but naturally, Brooklyn had waited until Elijah was gone to ask the hard questions.

Stalling for time, Hannah carefully slid the filled cookie sheet into the oven and started the timer, hoping inspiration would strike as she did.

"I know this is hard to keep in mind sometimes," she finally said once there was nothing left to do but to turn back towards Brooklyn, "but Dayton and Patrick were taught by their parents to think like that. It doesn't make it any easier to swallow because they're being jerks and no one likes being around that, but it's how they were raised. Hopefully, someday, they'll realize that it isn't right. In the meanwhile, the best thing you can do is be a good friend to Juan and stand up for him, but *not* by kicking Dayton in the shins when you do it."

Brooklyn had the good graces to look a little ashamed at that. "He's just such a jerk," she mumbled around the licking of her fingers clean. "He *likes* being mean."

The terrible part was, Brooklyn was spot on. Hannah couldn't say that out loud, of course, but yeah, Dayton had a mean streak in him a mile wide. She'd had hopes at the beginning of the year of bringing the class together as a whole, but it was nearing into March and they were just as fractured as ever, with Dayton – and Patrick as his sidekick – being a big part of that. It was the hardest class she'd ever had, and those two were the cause of about 97.2% of that heartache.

She was saved by Elijah's return just then, which thankfully kept her from having to come up with a suitable answer that didn't include, "Dayton was born mean as a rattlesnake and his parents have only made it worse."

She looked over at him coming through her front door and let out a little sigh of happiness. Not because she'd been saved from having to come up with some politically correct response to Brooklyn's thoughts, but rather because seeing him come through the front door...

It just *felt* right. Like it had happened a thousand times already, and would happen a thousand times more and it was just meant to be.

Elijah slung the gallon of milk up onto the counter as he popped a kiss onto Brooklyn's forehead, and then laid a kiss on Hannah that left her panting with lust by time he was done. They'd tried, in the beginning, to hide their relationship from Brooklyn, but...well, that had quickly died off. As Elijah had confessed to her one day, having Hannah in the same room as him and not kissing her was the purest form of torture God ever did create.

Elijah pulled back and cradled Hannah against his thighs, his arms wrapped around her waist as he stared down at her. "Hi honey, I'm home," he whispered with a naughty grin. She couldn't help it – she grinned back.

"I noticed," she whispered.

The timer for the cookies went off just then, and Elijah looked positively delighted. "Perfect timing, as always. My nose knows when it's time to eat. Brooksy, will you help a papa out by pulling them outta the oven?"

Together, they pulled the fat, golden cookies out of the oven and slid them onto the hot pads to protect the countertop, and then they all just breathed in deep.

"You're the best teacher *and* the best momma," Brooklyn said, her eyes shining bright with glee as she looked up at Hannah. The pain shot through her like a knife twisting through her heart. Having Brooklyn as her daughter would truly be a dream come true for her, but Sarah…?

Sarah would agree to that plan about the same time she agreed to chop off her right arm for funsies.

"Elijah—" Her voice broke from the pain and she cleared her throat and tried it again, pushing the pain down and burying it in her soul to be ignored like all of the other pain in her life. "Elijah, you want to pour us some milk while I dish out the cookies?"

She was bluntly sidestepping Brooklyn's comment. She knew what she wanted to say, and knew what she should probably say, and since she couldn't say the former and couldn't bring herself to say the latter, nothing at all was what she settled on. Luckily, Brooklyn's legendary attention span was no match against the tempting cookies in front of them, and she didn't even seem to notice Hannah's lack of an answer.

All too soon, it was time to drop Brooklyn off at home – another weekend together passing like a blur of fun and laughter and then always, the sadness at the end. Brooklyn threw her arms around Hannah's waist.

"I don't wanna go home," she cried with the passion that ten-year-old girls seemed to keep pent up inside at all times. "I wanna stay here with you. You don't never get drunk."

Hannah knelt down and hugged her back, the pain at Brooklyn's leaving ten times worse today because of those few words that said it all.

*You don't never get drunk.*

Words no ten year old should ever have to say.

"I know, sweetie," she whispered into Brooklyn's soft, shiny hair, feeling the hot burn of tears in her eyes as she hugged the little girl close. "It's hard. But we have to do what the courts say, at least for now. We'll figure something out, I promise. Please be careful, though – you know the rule."

"Don't say nothing to Sarah about you except that you're my teacher," Brooklyn recited dully, snuffling as she pulled back and wiped the backs of her hands across her tear-stained cheeks.

"I'm so sorry to ask you to do that," Hannah whispered, stroking Brooklyn's hair back out of her face. "I don't like you having to keep things from your mom—"

"She ain't my mom," Brooklyn broke in, shaking her head violently. "You are."

The sheer loyalty and love in her small form…she was Elijah's mini-me all right.

Again, Hannah sidestepped Brooklyn's words because it was her only choice, and what a terrible choice it was. "I love you, sweetie. I'll see you in class tomorrow as just one of my students, okay?"

Brooklyn nodded dully and, taking Elijah's hand, they left to do the bi-weekly drop-off at Sarah's house, leaving Hannah behind of course. The goodbyes were growing harder by leaps and bounds, and a small part of Hannah – that was getting bigger by the moment – wanted to grab up Brooklyn and Elijah and make a run for the border. Anything to keep from living through this constant pain.

As she set about putting the kitchen to rights, it hit Hannah anew why Elijah had been willing to take a job at the school just to be near his daughter. Brooklyn wasn't even Hannah's biological child, and she'd be willing to do something equally as extreme. She'd taught and loved on many students throughout the years, but Brooklyn…

She was like no other.

She heard the front door open but wasn't quick enough to wipe her tears away before Elijah spotted them. "Oh, Hannah," he murmured as he hurried over to the kitchen island and leaned against it, pulling Hannah up to cradle her against his strong thighs. "We'll figure something out," he promised her, echoing the words she'd used to reassure Brooklyn just minutes before. "This school year will come to an end and then we don't have to sneak around so much. A judge will listen…we'll be together as a family in no time at all."

She nodded listlessly against Elijah's chest, not able to find it in her to be more cheerful than that. Elijah tipped her chin up and smiled softly down at her, using the pad of his thumb to wipe her tears away. "Watching you with Brooksy…this is what I'd wanted all along. I didn't want to get married so early; I didn't want Brooksy. But once she was in my life, I never looked back. I couldn't look back. But I wanted something Sarah wasn't capable of, and it took us both a good long while to figure that out. But you and Brooksy…it's like God's giving me a second chance."

Something broke inside of Hannah just then, listening to this man in front of her talk about how much he loved his daughter. It was Hannah's weak spot – a man who loved children as much as she did. It almost seemed impossible.

And so she broke and she did what she'd been telling herself for months that she wouldn't do – she threw herself at Elijah.

Not literally, of course – she was already standing in the circle of his arms. Throwing herself at him would be a little more violent than the situation really called for. But every bit of restraint she'd gathered around herself for the last several months, every bit of willpower…it simply disappeared like it had never existed.

For the first time in her 34 years on this earth, she was the aggressor. She rose up on her tiptoes and shoved her hands into his thick dark hair and pulled him down to her, her mouth eating him up hungrily. He stiffened from surprise and she wondered for a moment if she'd made a mistake – if he wasn't attracted to her like she was to him.

But he began moaning with delight and lust as he nestled her closer against him, his penis quickly hardening against her belly, and she decided that for once, it'd been okay to take a chance.

Thinking became a really hard thing to do when he swung

her up onto the counter, a wide graceful arc that had her shouting with surprise and laughter as he grinned naughtily at her. They were eye to eye now, which made the idea of saying no, of moving away and being a good little girl, all the more impossible to fathom. Yeah, maybe according to society, they shouldn't be together. They certainly shouldn't be doing what every fiber of Hannah's being wanted them to do.

But she'd been breaking the rules all this time simply by dating Elijah, even if they hadn't actually had sex, and nothing bad had happened. In fact, it had been the best months of Hannah's life. So taking that next step and being together with the one man who set her world on fire…well, it didn't seem like such a terrible thing to do anymore.

Either she'd actually become more defiant and brave because of Elijah, or lust was addling her brain to the point where it couldn't figure out right from wrong. It could be either, really, and in that moment, Hannah found she didn't care which it was.

And that was the strangest, most thrilling part of all.

# CHAPTER 26

## ELIJAH

H<sup></sup>E'D NEVER SEEN Hannah like this before. Oh, he'd had dreams of her being wild and free and tearing at his hair as she moaned with lust, but those were just dreams. He'd never expected to actually see her do that.

But when she wrapped her thighs around him and pleaded with him to make love to her, all of his good sense went flying right out the window. The last two months of his life, he thought he was gonna go plumb crazy. Seeing her at school. Pulling in behind her house and parking in her backyard so no one could see him coming over. Not being able to claim her in public and walk down the street with her hand-in-hand…it had been a real test of his self-control and more than once, he was just sure he was gonna fail that test.

But now? He was failing spectacularly. He wasn't supposed to be picking Hannah up and carrying her down the hallway to her bedroom and spreading her out on the bed like a feast for the eyes.

He wasn't supposed to be, but he was anyway.

"Please, Elijah, please," Hannah mumbled, her head tossing back and forth on the pillow, her dark red hair going every which way. He slipped his fingers underneath the waistband of her yoga pants – her comfy weekend outfit, as she called it – but watching her walk around in skintight pants, following every curve of her body faithfully...

He was damn lucky he hadn't gone blind with lust over the past two months. She had every curve a man could want or ever dream of. She'd done a real good job of hiding those curves the first 34 years of her life, underneath baggy clothes and tied-back hair and thick glasses, but he'd found the real her, and he wasn't gonna let her go.

He peeled her yoga pants off, revealing creamy white legs just begging to be kissed, so kiss 'em he did. He started down at her ankles and moved up the sexiest pair of legs he was ever lucky enough to touch; muscular from horse riding but not in a weird bodybuilder way.

"Hannah, Hannah, Hannah," he moaned senselessly, his whole world disappearing with only these gorgeous legs left. He got up to the top of her thighs and sighed with happiness. She had these bright red curls that he couldn't help but nose and breathe in deep 'cause *damn* did she smell good. The world was going dark around the edges and she was moaning and trembling, and he was gonna bust a nut if he didn't come real quick. He'd been waiting a real long time for this; he'd been enduring the longest dry spell any red-blooded male could stand before going crazy, but finally, *finally* it was about to be over with.

He moved up over her, not sure if he was gonna lick her tits or move onto the grand finale and do a better job the second time 'cause Lordy, he needed some relief—

Except she wasn't moaning and trembling 'cause she was happy.

Not unless she had the world's weirdest way of showing that she was happy.

"Hannah?" he whispered, trying to figure out what in the hell was going on. She had tears running down her cheeks and she was shaking like a leaf, her head tossing just like before but this time, she was murmuring, "No, no, no, no," with her hands pushing at his shoulders, pushing him off her.

His lust-filled brain was having a real hard time keeping up. She'd been loving it.

Hadn't she?

She had wanted this.

Right?

He felt like he was going crazy.

"Hannah," he whispered again, stroking her cheek, "what's wrong? Did I hurt you?" He couldn't figure how he would have, considering he hadn't even been inside of her yet – something his dick was all too aware of – but maybe she was delicate in weird places or something.

She shook her head violently, her hair mixing with her tears and everything sticking every which way across her face, making a tangled mess and hiding her from him. He reached out and tried to brush her hair away from her face but she flinched, yanking away from him with a tiny mangled cry. She curled up in a ball, her back to him, as she sobbed so quietly, he wouldn't have known she was if he hadn't been paying attention.

His dick, which'd been hard enough to jackhammer through concrete just minutes before, deflated as he stared at the curve of Hannah's back. Her long red hair, all tangled and flowing this way and that, was a real pretty contrast to the cream of her skin, and was something he'd just stare at and enjoy…if she wasn't bawling like a baby.

He scrambled back through his memory, trying to think of a reason for the crying – any reason at all. Maybe his toenails were too long, and he stuck her with 'em. He looked down at his crooked toes, not a one of them going in a straight line, but nope, his toenails were all trimmed up. He'd just cut 'em a couple of nights ago. Plus, she wasn't yelling, "Ow! You stabbed me with your crooked toes!" or grabbing her legs in pain.

If he had to make a guess – and to be honest, girl feelings

were about as alien as New York City – he'd say her crying was from emotional pain, not physical. He was pretty hot to trot there for a bit, but he was also real sure that he would've noticed if he'd somehow skewered her with his toenails or put an elbow into her belly or something.

Plus, if she was hurt 'cause he did something to her, she woulda at least gone, "Oomph!" or "Ouch!" or "Hey, shithead, that was my ribcage!" or something.

Her shoulders weren't shaking quite so much, so Elijah dared to reach out to touch one. "Hannah?" he whispered again. "You…you wanna tell me what's going on?" She flinched when his fingertips brushed against her skin, but then, she did the damnedest thing – she scooted backwards just a titch so as to put her skin against his fingers again.

*Huh.*

He experimented a bit by opening up his hand and cupping her shoulder with it. Not only did she not tell him which bridge to jump off of, but she snuggled into him just a smidge bit more.

*Well, at least we're making progress.*

He decided to get brave and snuggle up against her backside, spooning her like he used to with Sarah. Draping his arm around her tiny waist and pulling her towards him, he realized how much he'd missed this. It'd been years and years and years since he'd spooned with a woman, and there wasn't any part of him that wasn't loving it.

Nope, no part at all.

*You can just quit that right now. Hannah's about 14 seconds away from bawling her head off again. She doesn't need a randy boy pawing at her.*

"Igstory," she mumbled into what had to be a very soggy pillow.

She was speaking, which was progress, but not real great progress, considering it wasn't English.

"What?" he said, stroking her wet hair away from her cheek.

How one person could produce this much moisture was beyond him.

"I didn't mean to cry," she said, and at least that time it was English she was speaking, although she wasn't making a lotta sense.

"I figure most tears aren't on purpose," he said seriously. "Wanna tell me what those tears were all about?"

She started shivering again, and he realized that without the heat of lovemaking to keep 'em warm, it was getting a might bit nippy, especially since they were buck naked. He reached down to the foot of the bed where they'd shoved the comforter when they'd begun having their fun, and pulled it up over them. She snuggled back against him again with a happy sigh.

"Thank you," she murmured. "That's much better."

He wrapped his arm around her, fitting nicely into the curve of her waist and up between her tits, and then didn't move another inch. "I don't wanna push you," he said softly, "but it seems to me that you got something you need to talk about. You feeling up to telling me?"

She shook her head violently, paused for a moment, and then nodded slowly. "I don't want to," she said seriously, as if that was some sorta shock to him, "but you're right, I need to. I thought…" She blew out a breath. "I thought I'd gotten over it. I mean, it's been thirteen years. That's plenty of time. Except, you were on top of me and I was back there again and…"

She stopped.

His mind spun. She hadn't actually said the words, of course, but it sure sounded like she was talking about rape. Nothing much else made sense. Why else would she be freaking out about him being on top of her?

"Who was the son of a bitch?" he snarled, his body going rigid with anger. "Who was the slimy bastard?"

"I'd come home for the summer," she answered, as if that was a damn answer to anything. "I had one year left in college, and then I could come back to Sawyer to teach. I was home on summer break – I guess I already said that, didn't I?" She blew out a breath of frustration. "It was the 4th of July. That's always been one of my favorite holidays – the fireworks going off, the smell of black powder in the air…there's nothing that screams holiday and summer and fun like a huge fireworks show. I was walking up the hill towards the city park, going to meet Dad, when suddenly I was being pulled into the trees. You know that line of poplars along the back side of the park?"

"Yeah," he whispered, imagining it all in his head clearly. Those poplars were the favorite of every horny teenager in Long Valley; in fact – and he'd die before he admitted it to Hannah – he was pretty damn sure that's where Brooksy was conceived. With the slope of the hill and how bushy the city let the poplars grow, it was about as private as you could get outside of a hotel room.

"He…he pulled me in there. Wrapped his hand across my mouth and told me to shush my crying. So I did. I didn't fight him. I didn't scream. I didn't slap him or knee him in the balls. I just lay there and stared up at the dark sky and listened to the fireworks boom and everyone cheer and clap, and wished I was dead. A part of me felt dead. I don't remember what I was wearing, or what he was wearing. The focus of the whole world…I don't know how to describe. Things just aren't there for me. I don't even know how long it lasted. And I sure don't know why I didn't fight back. He told me that I must want it – that's why I wasn't fighting him. I didn't believe him – of *course* I didn't want it – but it's always haunted me. Whenever I'm forced to think about that night, I have to wonder who that Hannah was. Of course you don't just lie there and take it. I would *never* do something like that. But I did. And I don't know why." Her voice was broken and reedy and thin as she finished whispering the worst story Elijah had ever heard.

"Did you tell your dad or the police or anybody?" He was sure he knew the answer, but he had to ask anyway.

She shook her head, still facing away from him. "No," she

whispered, and hiccuped. "He told me no one would believe me over him. Plus, it would ruin my career as a teacher. He promised me that I'd never get hired if word of this got out, and he was right.

"So, I went home and cleaned up and hid in bed under the blankets and then told my dad the next morning that I'd gotten a headache and that's why I didn't go watch the fireworks. He could tell I wasn't telling the truth, but...Dad was good at not pushing when you didn't want him to. So he left it alone."

"I don't get it," Elijah said slowly. "How would being raped hurt your career as a teacher? It wasn't like you'd asked for it to happen. No school would hold that against you."

"They would if your rapist was the teenage son of the judge in town." She said the words simply, as if stating the earth were round or the sky were blue.

*Teenage? Son of the judge?*

*Good Lord above, she's talking about Richard Schmidt.*

# CHAPTER 27
## HANNAH

S HE KNEW the moment that he'd figured out who'd raped her. He'd been slowly stroking her arm and hair, trying to suppress the anger she could feel roiling below the surface, and then he went stiff as a board.

"Richard Schmidt raped you?" he whispered, and she could feel him against her back, shaking from the shock of it all. "But, but," he sputtered, "he's two years younger than me. He woulda only been what, 15, 16 years old at the time?"

This.

This was why she hadn't ever told anyone what had happened. Blaming a 15-year-old boy – "I'll be 16 next month," he'd boasted to her as he'd dropped his pants – of raping her…

It was ludicrous.

Then add into the equation that he was the beloved and coddled son of the judge in town who believed he could do no wrong…

It would've been suicide for her to tell anyone.

But it was especially stupid of her to tell Elijah. He'd liked her and look at what she'd gone and done. Just like she'd expected, he didn't believe her.

*Stupid Hannah. Stupid, stupid. You never should've told him the truth. You should've made up some story —*

Her anger, boiling at a low simmer for the last thirteen years, overflowed and directed itself straight at Elijah Morland.

"Yeah, Richard Schmidt," she said sarcastically. "And you want to know what really chaps my butt? The fact that you seem to think that just because he was a teenage boy at the time, that he wasn't capable of rape. Well guess what, bucko, that's exactly why I didn't tell a single soul what had happened. I'd already been raped once. I didn't need to be raped by public opinion, too." She flipped over to face him and began shoving at his chest with all her might.

Well, pounding on it, if she was going to be honest about it. Pounding and hitting and scratching.

"He knew I was going to become a teacher!" she yelled. "He laughed at me while he was pushing away on top of me. Laughed and laughed. Told me that if I went to the police, that he'd tell them that I spent months trying to seduce him. As if I wanted his scrawny dick anywhere near me! But I'd be finished as a teacher – finished before I even started!"

And then she was sobbing again, when she'd just been sure she'd cried every bit of moisture out of her – apparently, she still had some left. She was hiccuping and her head ached from the force of her tears and her eyes burned from the pain pouring out of her and she hated, hated, *hated* Elijah in that moment. Hated him for prying the story out of her for the first time in her life; hated him for not believing her.

So, she told him that.

No, she *shouted* it at him. Calm, sweet, quiet Hannah who wouldn't say boo if her life depended on it – yeah, she yelled.

And it felt great.

"I! Hate! You!" she shouted, pounding on his chest with each word. She was shaking with anger and pain and no doubt snot would be dripping off the ceiling after she was done, but she couldn't calm down.

Wouldn't, wouldn't, wouldn't.

She realized then, in some dim and distant part of her mind, that Elijah was talking. She hadn't heard him say anything over the rushing of hatred through her veins, and she wondered for a moment how long he'd been speaking.

"What?" she asked dully.

She was going to throw him out of her bed. It was her house – she would make him leave. Tell him she never wanted to see him again. He could clean her classroom after she was gone for the day. Or wear a ski mask while he cleaned her room so she wouldn't have to look at his rotten, lowdown, pile-of-cow-poop face.

"I'd always known that Richard was trouble," he said, slow and quiet, stroking her hair out of her face again. Long and tangled and a pain in the rear as usual, it'd gotten stuck to her copious snot and tears, and she was sure that there was no one on the planet who was less sexy than her in that moment, but she didn't care. She didn't give a rotten fig leaf if she was the ugliest woman on earth. He caused this. He could darn well stare at it. "I also knew he liked to push the girls. Even two years younger than me, I was always hearing him bragging up a storm 'bout getting girls to do what he wanted. I didn't know that he pushed the line that far, though. I...I can't imagine what you went through. How hard it must've been, especially since you couldn't tell anyone. Damn, you were real lucky he didn't get you pregnant."

She settled down into her soaked pillow, still facing his direction but refusing to meet his gaze. "I cried again when I started my period two weeks later. Tears of joy, which was a nice change of pace for me at that point." She laughed bitterly. "If I'd ended up pregnant...I don't have a clue what I would've done. Not one. I don't like abortion, but giving birth to the baby of my rapist, plus he was underage...my life would've been ruined. Destroyed. Yeah, I was really lucky he didn't get me pregnant."

They were silent then, just letting the weight of the truth settle out over them.

The gushing anger that had propelled her towards shouting at Elijah was gone. She just felt...numb. Like there was some opaque filmy barrier between her and the rest of the world. She was moving slowly through the sludge and mud, not sure if she ever wanted to speak or think or breathe again, when she remembered something he'd asked her about a while ago, which she'd been mulling around ever since. It'd taken her a good long while to figure out why she'd hated his question so much, or rather, face the truth of why she did. A part of her had known; she just didn't want to admit to it.

"A while back, you asked me about why I wasn't wearing glasses in my high school senior photo," she said in a robotic voice, still not looking at him. Maybe she'd never look at him again. That seemed like a real good plan in that moment. "I probably surprised you with how I responded, since it was an innocent question. But it was skirting painfully close to the biggest secret of my life, and I didn't want you anywhere near that sore spot."

She heaved a big sigh. "I wouldn't have admitted to it at the time, but I started wearing those thick glasses as armor against the world. After that night...I went down to Dr. Mor and told him that I wanted to wear glasses because contacts were just too much work. Then I asked for the thickest lens he had; they can thin them out now so even the most blind among us don't have to look like we're peering through a funhouse mirror at the county fair, but I wanted them thick. I stopped wearing any makeup at all; I stopped curling my hair; I stopped even wearing my hair down. The uglier I was, the less likely it was that someone would jump out and grab me. No one wants to rape an ugly chick."

"But you changed this year," he said, cupping one of her hands in his and bringing it up to his mouth to kiss. "You're damn beautiful."

"I was taking a chance on you," she admitted, mustering up the courage to look at him for just a moment, and then her eyes dropped back down and she was staring at their hands, folded together between them, tanned roughened skin against the painful whiteness of hers. There was a strange kind of rightness to the sight – that the differences showed that they belonged together, instead of proving how wrong they were for each other. "Michelle and Carla…they pushed me every step of the way. They don't know – no one does except now you, and Richard, I guess. Unless alcohol has pickled his brain to the point that he doesn't remember anymore. Always a possibility," she said dryly. He didn't earn the title of town drunk by being a teetotaler, that was for sure. "But Michelle and Carla – after years of being my friends, they just thought that I was shy and needed help figuring out how to wear makeup and put in contacts. And, spoiler alert, I am shy, and I did need help learning how to wear makeup." She laughed a little at that, and he joined her, pulling her up against his strong chest and cuddling her there.

She waited for the panic to come – the suffocating feeling that she was going to die or (even worse in her estimation) be hurt and not be able to stop it – but…it didn't come. They'd cuddled a lot over the past few months, and it'd never caused her to have a meltdown before, but after the worst attempted round of sex in the history of mankind, it was hard to take anything for granted.

*So it's only sex that causes me to lose my ever lovin' mind. Good to know.*

"Your disguise sure worked on me for a long time," Elijah admitted, freeing one of his hands so he could stroke down her shoulder and side in long, even strokes. "You were just Miss Lambert. I knew who you were, but I didn't pay attention beyond that. But then…I don't know. One day, I just saw you – the real you. You weren't just the teacher, there but not someone to pay attention to. You were beautiful, even with your hair pulled straight back and not a stitch of makeup on. Although, I do love your hair – you should never pull it back in a bun and hide it again. I could do nothing but play with your hair for the rest of my life, and die a happy man."

She laughed a little at that, but he rushed on. "I mean it," he insisted. "You don't just have red hair. It's red with bits of gold in it, like sunshine took up residence in your hair or something. It isn't ever the same – depending on the light, it's dark red or strawberry red or golden or almost black – I've never seen anything like it."

"I thought you said you weren't a romantic," she reminded him with a light laugh, scrubbing at the dried tears on her cheeks. Laughing, even a little…it felt nice. Real nice. "Sunshine taking up residence in my hair sure sounds romantic to me."

His mouth twisted up as he thought about it. "You might be right," he finally admitted. "I thought romance was for fools. After everything with Sarah, it was real hard to believe that I was ever gonna find love. The best I was a-hopin' for was sex. Love was just something the country singers sing about to make money. It wasn't real. But…" He stared straight into her eyes, his gray-green eyes serious, like he was saying the most important statement of his life, "I was wrong. Hannah, I love you like I've never loved anyone in my life."

She teared up then – happy tears – and opened up her mouth to speak, when he lightly placed a finger on her lips to stop her. "I need to say all of this 'cause you gotta know. I'm sorry I scared you earlier. I'm sorry you didn't feel like I was taking you seriously or thinking that you were lying to me about Richard. You weren't. You don't have a lying bone in your body. Plus, the way you were crying…no one can fake cry that hard. Hell, Sarah fake cried on me a lot over the years, knowing I'd hate to see her tearing up, but after a while, I started to realize when they were crocodile tears, and when they were real tears. Earlier tonight, those tears you were spilling were as real as they get."

*He loves me…he loves me!*

In all her life, Hannah had had one male say that he loved her, and that had been her father. Hearing Elijah say the words – it set her world on fire.

She stroked his stubbled cheek, looking into his gray-green eyes that were looking back steadily, waiting patiently for her to speak. "I want to…well, you know." She waved her hand around to indicate their bodies, too embarrassed to say the word 'sex' out loud. Which was stupid, because she'd just finished discussing rape with Elijah, but still…she wasn't used to talking about this sort of thing with anyone at all, let alone a male. "I just don't know how. When you were on top of me, I was at the park again and I couldn't breathe and…" She trailed off. "I want to, I really do. Please have patience with me, though."

His fingers were drawing lazy circles on her skin as he spoke softly. "Hannah, I haven't had sex in years. A little more of a wait isn't gonna kill me, no matter what my ball sac says." She choked on an embarrassed laugh at that, her cheeks blazing a brilliant red at his words. Sure, she was lying naked in the circle of his arms, but that didn't mean she was used to this sort of thing. "I don't know how much porn you've watched or naughty stories you've read over the years, but me laying on top of you isn't the only way we can do this, and considering what Dickwad did, I'm thinking it surely isn't the best way, at least not right now." She snorted a little at the name 'Dickwad' and he grinned at her, pleased as punch with himself. "Did you see what I did there?" he asked with a wink. "He's a dickwad for sure, but his name is also Richard, so…"

"Yeah, I caught that," she said dryly, wanting him to move on to the part where they discussed different sex positions. She wasn't about to actually answer his rhetorical question, but no, she'd never watched porn or read 'naughty stories,' as he put it. Her knowledge of sex was what little she'd gleaned while listening to others talk about it in whispered voices. Most people wouldn't believe that a 34-year-old woman could be as ignorant as she was, but then again, even Hannah knew her story wasn't a normal one.

*Thanks, Dickwad.*

"So, I think we oughta try me just lying here, as still as a stone, and you can do what you like to me." He rolled over onto his back and put his hands down by his side, even closing his eyes so he wasn't intimidating her by watching her every movement.

Still, he was a guy and he was naked and he wanted her to "do what she wanted" to him, which officially made him the most intimidating person on the face of the planet. She sat up cross-legged next to him and looked down at his body, not really sure what to do. Her dad had always been a modest guy, so he'd worn an undershirt even around the house or while out swimming. She couldn't remember a time when she'd even seen his chest, let alone the rest of him.

And Dickwad – she was sure growing to love that name for him – well, that didn't even bear thinking about. She surely hadn't laid there and explored his body carefully while he raped her.

But even as she hesitated, Elijah didn't move a muscle. He didn't demand that she hurry up; he didn't even give her any pointers, which honestly, she rather wished he would. He just lay there, still as a stone as promised, and waited.

So, she took a deep breath and reached out her right hand to stroke up his side. His skin was soft, over the muscles of his—

He began shaking under her touch and horrified, her eyes flew up to his. "You're tickling me," he gritted out, his eyes firmly clamped shut. "It's fine; I just...my sides are ticklish, is all."

"I didn't know," she said apologetically. Mylanta, it was just like her to go for sexy and instead end up tickling the man. Weren't there manuals for this sort of thing that she could read and study up on so she didn't end up making such a fool of herself?

"I know, and like I said, it's okay. Nothing you do is wrong. I'm just a-lyin' here. You do what you like."

She bit down on her bottom lip with a silent groan. She didn't know what she liked, though. She wished they'd start with what he liked, except…well, he'd tried that, hadn't he, and she'd ended up curled up in a ball, sobbing hysterically.

She fought back the desire to ask him what to do, and instead forced herself to touch his pecs instead, staying far away from his ticklish sides. His flat nipples hardened up at her touch, and so she ran her fingertips over them, interested to see what they felt like, and heard a quiet groan as she did so. Worried, her eyes flew back up to his, but even as naïve and ignorant as she was, she knew that wasn't a look of pain on his face.

He was liking it. He was liking her touch.

Emboldened, she leaned over and licked the hard nipple. He groaned louder this time and she felt a silly little grin cross her face. Maybe she wasn't the world's worst lover after all. So she tried wrapping her lips around his nipple and sucking, which was when he bucked his hips. Just once and then he lay there, not moving a muscle. She pulled back worriedly anyway and studied his face.

His face that was covered with sweat from the effort of keeping still; his fists balled by his sides as he fought himself not to reach for her.

This time, she smirked. She, Worst Lover Ever, was driving Elijah nuts.

Yeah, she didn't mind this one bit.

# CHAPTER 28

## ELIJAH

THIS WAS EITHER the worst idea he'd ever come up with, or the best. It'd be the best one if he managed to live through it, but at the moment…

She was slowly but surely driving him insane.

It wasn't a fact he'd brag about in the men's locker room, that was for damn sure, but the truth of the matter was, he'd only ever slept with one person. He'd lost his virginity to Sarah, who'd been with plenty of guys before him and knew just what she liked and how she liked it. She'd bluntly bossed him around in the bedroom, making sure he did everything she wanted, and…well, that never changed.

But the stop 'n go of tonight, after the longest dry spell of his life, and now Hannah exploring him without him able to do a thing in return…

Definitely the worst idea ever.

Her warm breath washed over his dick as she shifted her weight to explore his legs, and Elijah wasn't sure if he wanted to scream or cry. He counted back from ten to one as she wrapped her soft fingers around his dick, then twenty-five to one as she probed it like you would a slab of meat on your plate. He quickly moved onto singing nursery songs – strangely, the only song he could think of at the moment was *Mary Had a Little Lamb* – as her fingers drifted up and down the hardest hard-on he'd ever had in his life.

*Fleece was white as snoooooooowwwwwww…*

He screwed his eyes shut, panting. He was gonna come. There was no way he'd be able to stop it. She didn't have the slightest idea of what she was doing, and instead of being a turn-off, his dick was loving every bit of it.

It washed over him – his back was arching and he couldn't breathe or see or think but just feel the relief in his nut sac as his cum shot outta him.

Finally, the world came back into focus and he blearily opened his eyes to peer up at Hannah, fascination and horror warring openly on her face. "Is that what happens when a male ejaculates?" she whispered.

He laughed a little even as his body eased back into the mattress.

"I—I'm not laughing at you," he said quickly, before she could get all riled up on him. "Just, uh, your words. Ummm… yeah, that's what happens when a male ejaculates." He repeated her formal wording, his mouth twitching as he said it. He wasn't the most practiced guy on the planet, but compared to her, he was practically a manwhore. "Usually, I'd be doing it inside of you, but it's been a real long time since I've had anyone helping me along except me, and…I lost control. I'm sorry."

She nodded as if she was understanding him, and then licked hesitantly at the cum that'd happened to land on her hand. "I always wondered what it tasted like," she said matter-of-factly after she ran her tongue across the white blob. Elijah felt the offer practically strangle him in an effort to tumble off his tongue – *I'll let you taste mine anytime you want* – but swallowed.

Hard.

He looked around her bedroom for a box of Kleenexes to

clean up the mess when her next words stopped him short. "So, the longer you go between ejaculations, the harder it is to keep from ejaculating?"

She sounded like a student in some sorta bizarre sex class, where he was the teacher, and…well, he was back to the best / worst conundrum from before. He spotted a tissue box on her dresser and swung outta bed and over to the box to wipe up, hoping to come up with something that sounded good by time he was done.

Finally, he had no excuse left, and he turned back to see Hannah still cross-legged on the bed, naked as a jaybird, as if that was a normal state of being for her. He felt a bolt of lust shoot through him, and could only be thankful that he'd already come. Looking at Hannah sitting like that – if he hadn't already found relief, that sight would've pushed him over the edge.

He focused on her kneecaps, hoping the sight would help him calm down some. "Yeah," he finally said in answer to her question. "The longer the wait, the harder it is to wait." He sent her a rueful grin. "It'll be a while before my friend here is ready to go again, but that just means that it won't be so hard to lie still."

He went to crawl back into position, hoping his words were right and he would be able to wait longer this time, when she put out her hand to stop him. "It was fun to explore, truly, but… I think I'm ready for you to explore back."

Her words were brave, but he'd bet his left nut on the fact that it was a front. She was dad-blamed terrified and just one hair away from shaking like a leaf again.

He hesitated, trying to figure the best way to make it work for her, and then hit on it.

"Okay, you lie right here," he pulled her onto her side so she was facing him, "and I'll lie right here." He stretched out next to her so they were face-to-face. "That way, I'm not on top of you, hurting you or making you panic." He paused for a second and then asked, "You're fine like this, right?"

She smiled a wavery smile at him. "Yeah. I'm good. I'll…I'll tell you if that changes." She looked like a spooked colt, 'bout ready to take off for the hills, but Elijah decided that it was best to take her at her word. Not to mention that not touching her was an unbearable thought. Even though his dick was limp for the moment, he could already tell it wasn't gonna last long that way.

He stroked down her arm and over one tit and then the other. Her nipples, all pink and sweet-looking, puckered right up, just looking like they were begging to be kissed. Her breath got quick and he looked up at her face to find it all scrunched up. He stopped and pulled his hand away slowly, trying not to jerk and spook her. Her eyes fluttered open and she smiled dreamily at him. "No wonder you liked it when I…" She trailed off and gestured at his chest.

He lay still as a log and just looked at her, silently prompting her to actually say the words. She would only become less squeamish about sex if she learned it was okay to say her thoughts out loud.

"When I licked your nipples," she whispered, a blush covering her from head to toe.

He grinned at her, pleased as punch with her bravery. "Every person is different, of course, but I've always had me some real sensitive nips," he told her. "Your mouth on them is about as good a feeling as your mouth on my dick."

She looked a little green around the edges at that thought. "You want me to put my mouth on…that?" she asked faintly.

"Not if you don't want to," he said, shrugging. "And you don't have to do it every time, even if you end up liking it. You only have to do what feels good. There's only one rule for the bedroom, and that's it. Nothing else matters."

She nodded seriously, and then began cautiously exploring him with her hands and fingertips, just as he explored every dip and curve of her body. He'd done enough sightseeing down at the lake and watched enough porn to know that every girl was built differently, but still, it was a little crazy to him just how different she was from Sarah. Her tits were heavy, like they were weighed down by something, and were a bit longer, making it easy for him to wrap his hands around them.

Then there was the soft belly – she had a real skinny waist, but a small pouch in her belly, keeping her from turning into a bag o' bones that poked him with every move. Being a girl, Elijah was real sure that she hated that pouch, but damn, he loved it.

Not as much as he loved the curls and smell of her, though. He had never smelled something that good. Watching her face closely for any signs of panic, he reached down and stroked his fingers over her mound. She groaned – just a little moan of delight – and he grinned to himself. A far cry from shaking and crying hysterically, that was for damn sure. He stroked his fingers over and between the lips of her pussy. His hands were roughened from years of manual labor, so he kept a close eye on her to make sure he didn't hurt her with a jagged fingernail or something, but all he saw was pleasure.

She began bucking her hips in that age-old request for him to come inside her – she probably didn't even realize what she was doing or what it meant. But her body knew.

He wanted to roll over on top of her and push himself inside and feel her warmth around him and—

He forced himself to stop. Just thinking about it was a real good way to torture himself. It wasn't an option, at least not right now.

"Hannah," he whispered, and her golden eyelashes fluttered open.

"Yeah?" Her voice was all trembly, just like her body, but this time it was with need, not fear. He'd done good, and now it was time for him to show her that him being inside of her was a good thing. He snagged a condom out of his wallet and rolled it down into place.

"Okay, I'm gonna roll over onto my back," he said as he did it, "and you're gonna get up on top of me and straddle me. Lower yourself real slow." He helped her into position, his fingers gripping the tiniest waist he'd ever seen on a grown woman, and then guided her down his dick nice and slow. The world went black for a moment and he thought he was about to make an ass outta himself by coming too quickly twice in one night, but he pushed the lust down. *Not yet, you jackass.* "Move your knees so you're kneeling…there. Perfect. Now, you're gonna move up and down, and I'll help you."

She had a bit of sweat on her forehead as she concentrated with every inch of her body, wanting to do it "right," still not convinced that there wasn't a wrong, but the longer they went, the less…constipated she looked.

Finally, she met his eyes with a whoop of triumph. "It's like riding a horse!" she exclaimed.

He laughed through his lust. "That's a real good description," he told her, his own forehead beading up with sweat. Letting her take the lead, trying to hold back for as long as possible…it was gonna be the death of him, he was sure of it. Her rhythm was getting better as she went on, and it just felt so damn good…

He screwed his eyes tight as he tried to force the lust down and not come again but it was all too much, it felt too good, and then she was squeezing him hard and yelling about something but he couldn't listen, he could only feel himself spilling inside of her and the joy of finally coming inside of a woman for the first time in a real long time…

His eyes slowly drifted open and he looked down at her head, nestled against his chest where she'd collapsed, breathing like she'd run the 100-meter or something. He reached up and stroked her hair away from her face. "How was that?" he whispered.

She pulled away from him, sweat making 'em stick together, and grinned. "A part of me had known that having sex couldn't possibly be what it was like with Dickwad, or people wouldn't be doing it all of the time. But it was the only kind of sex I'd ever had, and I just couldn't figure out how you could make it nice enough to want to do it again and again.

"Thinking about it over the last several months, I'd finally decided that I'd do it for you. It'd hurt because I was obviously built wrong, but maybe it wouldn't hurt quite as much as it did with Dickwad, and it'd be worth it if it'd make you happy. It was so scary to do it, though, and now…It's like jumping into a mountain lake and expecting it to be ice cold, but instead it's nice and warm like you've jumped into a bathtub. The shock of it feeling good makes it almost too hard to really understand what's going on."

He gently rolled her on over to her side, treating her like he would a piece of glass, and began stroking her hair away from her face. "There are lots of different positions for sex," he whispered. "If we ever try one or I do something that you don't like, you gotta tell me. The last thing I ever wanna do is hurt you. Sex should always make you feel good – nothing else. There isn't a damn thing wrong with you. Dickwad was just living up to his name, is all."

She laughed lightly at that, even as her eyelids began to drift shut. "I promise I'll tell you. Now that I know how wonderful it's supposed to feel…" Her eyelids fluttered open and she grinned naughtily at him. "I won't put up with anything less."

He let out a deep laugh at that. "I like your thinking," he said approvingly. He nestled her close to him and together, they drifted off to sleep.

# CHAPTER 29

## ELIJAH

VEN THE ALARM CLOCK going off couldn't upset him.

He slowly drifted awake, his arm wrapped snugly around Hannah's waist, and slapped at his phone without even opening his eyes.

He may not have his eyes open, but he sure could manage a grin.

A big, shit-eating grin.

He figured after last night, he deserved the biggest, most shit-eating grin any red-blooded male had ever grinned.

Hannah grumbled sleepily about the alarm clock going off, and then snuggled back against him as if she'd been sleeping in his arms every night for a decade, and this was the most normal thing in the world to be lying there with him.

With any luck at all, she would be sleeping in his arms for the next ten years, and then fifty more after that. The way he figured it, he deserved a run of good luck after years of nothing but Sarah in his life.

Regretting every moment of it, he pulled away from Hannah and forced himself to swing his legs outta bed and take on the day. After splashing some water on his face to help the waking-up process, he pulled his clothes on from the day before, dropped a kiss on the forehead of a sleeping Hannah, and then drove as quick as his ol' diesel would take him to his house out on the outskirts of Sawyer. He could take a Navy shower, put on some less wrinkled clothes, and then head back to the school with no one the wiser.

After a hurried breakfast of burnt toast and lots of coffee, he made it to school with three minutes to spare.

*Not bad. Not bad at all.*

He kept his eyes peeled for Brooksy or Hannah, hoping just to see one or the other of 'em as the morning passed. He was surprised by how quickly he started missing them. Going without them was starting to get painful, that was for damn sure.

*Only three more months until school is out and then no one can say a word about me dating Hannah.*

It was the only thing that kept him cheerful as he cleaned the boy's bathroom. How was it that boys never managed to hit the toilet? He was damn sure that when he was a kid, his aim was loads better than the kids nowadays. His parents woulda paddled his ass if he'd left yellow puddles behind every time he went pee.

It was a real good thing that both Brooksy and Hannah was at the school, or he would've quit a long time ago. Even working nights at the gas station and never sleeping right was better than cleaning up puddles of yellow piss.

A lifetime later or so, lunchtime finally hit and he sat with Brooksy, Juan, and Juniper, listening to them snigger 'bout some dumb joke that every student was telling each other that day. Juan would ask, "What has hundreds of ears but can't hear a thing?" and then Brooksy would yell out, "A cornfield!" and then all three of them would collapse into giggles.

Yup, it sure was a stupid joke, but he figured it was even funnier to them 'cause it was a room full of farming kids.

Watching the fifth graders acting like children – 'cause they *were* children, dammit – he had a hard time thinking that he was once their age. His parents didn't take kindly to dumb jokes or puns or anything that a kid would think was funny, so he'd grown up without much laughter around him.

Listening to Brooksy asking the lead-in line for the third time in a row, he had to admit that maybe there were something to his parents dislike of childish humor. It sure wasn't for him – not anymore. But, as Brooksy looked up at him, laughing uproariously as Juan shouted out, "A cornfield!" he decided that maybe it was okay. As long as Brooksy was happy, he was, too.

Although maybe he oughta buy her a joke book so she could switch things up every once in a while. Perhaps then she wouldn't be driving her papa to insanity quite so quickly.

Just as they were clearing their trays off the table so the kids could run off to the playground, one of the older lunch ladies – Miss Patsy with her nest of bright blue hair tucked up under her hairnet – slow-poked her way over to him. Her arthritis in her hips was giving her fits again today, he could tell, and he wondered again to himself why she didn't just take social security payments and stay at home. Somehow, she managed to always be cheerful, even when she was in lots of pain.

"Elijah, dear, can you come help us old ladies out? Why, Sue dropped a big bag of salt and busted it open all over the floor. It's a real mess in there now."

"Of course, Miss Patsy," he told her. He hugged Brooksy real quick and then followed Miss Patsy's slow, painful gait back into the kitchen. The lunch ladies were sure a nice bunch to let him eat every day for free, and he wasn't about to thank 'em for it by ignoring their requests for help.

Miss Patsy'd been right – the salt had gone everywhere. He was sure if he took the covers off the lights in the ceiling, he'd find it in there, too. He tried not to grumble too loudly as he took stock of the mess. He probably oughta sweep up the majority of it just to keep 'em from tracking it every which way, and then do a deep scrub of the walls and ceiling. He spotted a light coat of white across the tops of the ovens on the other side of the room, and knew then that he was in for it. He was gonna spend the rest of the afternoon right here.

*Better then yellow piss, right?*

But only just barely.

Sue kept apologizing to him. "I don't know how it happened," she fretted, wringing her hands as she watched him begin to methodically push the salt into a growing pile. "It was in my hands, and then it was going everywh—"

BEEP! BEEP! BEEP!

The ear-splitting, eye-watering fire alarm was so shocking, Miss Patsy threw her hands up in the air with a yell that was almost as loud as the alarm, sending a container of something or another flying across the kitchen, white stuff arcing behind it as it went.

Elijah stifled a half-laugh, half-groan.

He had job security, that was for damn sure.

He practically shoved the lunch ladies towards the row of jackets, ignoring their protests 'bout needing to clean up the mess they were leaving behind. "We gotta go, ladies!" he hollered above the racket. "It'll be here when we get back, I promise."

*Or it'll be burnt to a crisp, in which case it doesn't matter anyway.*

He kept that thought to himself. This wasn't a planned fire drill, and even if he couldn't smell smoke, that didn't mean a damn thing. It had to be here at the school somewhere, which made shivers go a-dancin' over his skin. What if it was in Hannah's classroom? What if she or Brooksy was hurt?

Leaving the squawking lunch ladies behind, he took the stairs to the main floor two at a time, snagging his jacket from his closet as he ran down the hallway. The classrooms were all empty and none had flames or smoke rolling outta them, so he kept going, running past the flashing lights and alarms loud enough to wake the dead.

*Gotta find Hannah and Brooksy. Hannah and Brooksy. Gotta make sure they're okay. Hannah and Brooksy.*

The alarms were quickly making him nuts – so loud, it was hard to remember his own name, let alone anything important. He burst out of the front doors of the school and pushed out through the crowd of kids, past a couple of the teachers, and hooked a right to find the line for Hannah's class. They were supposed to be lined up right next to the largest pine tree in the schoolyard, just like every other monthly fire drill they'd done that school year.

He caught sight of Hannah and he breathed a sigh of relief even as he realized that dammit all, she wasn't okay. Usually calm and keeping the kids calm too, today she was terrified, frantically counting heads as she stood next to the line of her students.

He took off at a loping run again, his legs pounding the frozen ground but just like in those nightmares he hated, Hannah didn't seem to be getting any closer, no matter how fast he ran or how hard he pushed himself. He darted past lines of kids and teachers yelling at their kids and the panic was just getting worse 'cause he was looking at the same line of students as Hannah was, and there was no Brooksy there.

It was an eternity, or maybe two, before he finally got to her side. "Where's Brooksy?" he demanded, even as he could plainly see there was no Brooksy in sight.

Panic and worry was making it hard for him to think. To breathe. He wanted to shake Hannah's shoulders until Brooksy appeared. He wanted to yell at her for losing his daughter. *Where's Brooksy? Where's Brooksy? Where's Broo—*

"I don't know," Hannah said, voice a-quivering. "We'd just sat down in our seats and I was starting to do the afternoon headcount when the fire alarm went off. But—" she looked up at him, her blue eyes swimming with tears, "I haven't seen her at all since the lunch bell rang."

Elijah turned to the line of students, huddled together against the bitter cold, and roared, "Any of you seen my Brooksy? Any of you seen my daughter?!"

As one, they all shook their heads. Elijah scanned the crowd, looking for Juan or Juniper. They'd both been there at lunch. Surely they would know where she was.

He caught Juan's eye, and Juan just shook his head, looking worried himself. "After we ate with you," he said, "she went off to turn in her library book. Said she had to get it in today or she'd be in trouble. She weren't in line when the bell rang."

The library. Of course. He'd find her in the library line. Wasn't that just like his daughter. Too smart for her own damn good, or for the good of his heart. He took off a-lopin' towards the librarian, the blaring of the fire alarm 'bout to drive him to drink. If they'd just turn that damn thing off, he could think.

He caught sight of Mrs. Damerell, her stooped shoulders rounding in on themselves in the bitter cold. She was standing next to the music teacher, but there weren't any children near her. "Mrs. Damerell!" he roared over the fire alarm. "Where's Brooksy?"

Mrs. Damerell peered at him through the beginning flakes of an incoming snowstorm. "Brooksy?" she repeated blankly, as if he'd started speaking Latin on her or something.

"Brooklyn Sarah Morland," he gritted out, emphasizing every syllable like he would when talking to someone on the slow side. He clenched his fists, fighting the overwhelming urge to hit something.

"Oh! Well, Brooklyn came in and turned in her library book," Mrs. Damerell yelled back over the racket, "but then she left. She wasn't in the library when the alarm went off. I was by myself."

But he'd already taken off towards the school secretary, Mrs.

Worsop. He was being rude, but he didn't give a flyin' duck's ass about that. All that mattered was Brooksy.

"Mrs. Worsop," he said, interrupting whatever it was that she was saying to Principal Zeller. "Did Brooksy get checked out of the office today?"

Mrs. Worsop let out an irritated *harrumph* at his impertinent interruption, but answered anyway. "No, she wasn't." Her eyes sharpened. "Is she missing?"

"She wasn't in Hannah's class after lunch," Elijah said, trying not to hyperventilate. He had to think straight. He had to just give 'em the facts. They'd know what to do. "I ate lunch with her like normal; she turned in a library book; and then she disappeared. No one has seen her since."

Mr. Zeller nodded and opened up his mouth to ask a question when the sound of sirens tore up the road and into the school parking lot. Chief Anderson, the new fire chief in town, had slapped a flashing yellow light on top of his bright green SUV and had turned on some sorta siren that made him sound like he was in a real fire truck. He jumped outta his personal vehicle, tapped some knob, and the light and siren turned off. *Thank God.* The fire alarm by itself was enough to drive a man to drink; adding in a siren too was gonna make him plumb loco.

"Do we have a fire?" Chief Anderson yelled as he headed in their direction. "I called dispatch and they said they didn't have a practice fire drill on the schedule today."

The principal shook his head. "It's not a practice fire drill, but no one has been able to smell smoke or see it, or flames for that matter. Mrs. Worsop and I were just talking about checking to see if some kid pulled a fire alarm to get out of class this afternoon when Elijah here told us that his daughter is missing."

Chief Anderson swung towards Elijah, his dark brown eyes steady. "Give me just one moment, and then we'll get to work on this, I promise," he told Elijah as he pulled his radio off his belt clip. "Calling all fire personnel," he said into the radio. "We have an unplanned fire alarm going off at the Cleveland Elementary School and a missing—" He pulled his thumb off the button. "What grade is your daughter in?"

"Fifth," Elijah said tersely, fighting the urge to yank the radio out of the man's hand and start bellowing into it. He wanted to do something – anything at all. Panic was flooding through him, pulsing, making his skin dance and jump.

"A missing fifth-grade girl has also been reported," the chief yelled into the radio, trying to be heard over that damn fire alarm. "All personnel who can respond, meet me here at the elementary school." He pulled his thumb away from the button and looked at the principal. "I was driving past on the way back from lunch," he shouted, "when I heard the alarms going off. I'm not dressed in my turnout gear because I wasn't expecting to fight a fire on the way back from lunch," he gave 'em a crooked grin, "but my men should be here soon, and they'll be suited up to go into the building." He turned to Elijah. "What does your daughter look like, and what's her name? Let's check each of the lines out here and make sure she isn't in the wrong line for some reason."

"Should I check surveillance tapes to see if a kid pulled the fire alarm?" the principal hollered over the noise at their retreating backs.

"No, sir," Chief Anderson hollered back respectfully, turning back to the principal even as he was continuing to walk away. "Let my guys get here and clear the school before you go back in. There'll be plenty of time to find out if it's a student pulling a prank, after we're sure it's safe."

The principal nodded begrudgingly as Elijah and Anderson took off at a trot, Elijah scrambling to remember what on earth his daughter had worn to school that day. The quickly thickening snow was making it hard to see ten feet in front of him, driving home the realization that no matter how much he loved his daughter, he couldn't protect her from everything. Not from this snow, and not from this fire.

It was the worst he'd ever felt in his whole life, even worse than when his parents had threatened to disown him for knocking up Sarah, or when Sarah had told him that she didn't have to pretend to love him anymore.

No, this was much, much worse than that. If he didn't find his daughter soon, he was sure he'd slowly lose his mind.

*Brooksy, where are you? I'm sorry I'm such a rotten papa. I'm sorry I lost you. I won't never screw up again. Just be okay.*

*Please.*

# CHAPTER 30
## HANNAH

HER USUALLY ORDERLY LINES of students had dissolved into clumps as their small bodies huddled together, trying to stay warm in what looked like an incoming blizzard. Hannah would normally be ordering the students back into line, but today, she shouted over the blaring alarm to push together tighter. Shared body heat was the only thing that would get them through this.

*If this is some student trying to get out of taking a test this afternoon, I hope their ears are frozen solid.*

She felt bad even thinking such a thing, but on the other hand, her own ears were frozen solid, so it did seem like just retribution.

Even as she hugged shaking, freezing students against her side, running her hands over their arms to try to keep them warm, she kept scanning the kids milling all about, hoping and praying that she'd spot Brooklyn's dark blonde hair swinging as she came running over, giving some excuse for why she'd been gone. Maybe she got stuck in the bathroom. Maybe she got scared and was hiding underneath a desk somewhere.

Maybe she'd been snatched, and the kidnapper pulled the fire alarm on the way out to cover his tracks and create chaos.

She swallowed down the bile in her throat. She couldn't panic. Not yet. Had anyone called Sarah to tell her that her daughter was missing? Hannah dreaded having to make the phone call – Sarah wasn't her favorite person on the best of days, and today was definitely *not* one of those – but she knew someone needed to. If she was Brooklyn's momma and no one had told her that her daughter had gone missing as soon as they knew there was a problem? Most adults who knew her didn't believe she could yell, but in that situation, she'd prove them dead wrong.

As it was, she wanted to yell and scream and throw a fit over Brooklyn being missing, but at who? And say what? Technically, Brooklyn had been under her supervision when she'd disappeared. She'd never shown up to class, sure, but she was supposed to, and she hadn't, and Hannah couldn't find her, and—

"Ouch!" Tahlia yelped and Hannah looked down in surprise to realize that she'd been squeezing the little girl's shoulder like she could force Brooklyn's safe return into existence by wringing it out of Tahlia.

"Sorry, Tahlia," she shouted over the blaring of the alarm. If someone didn't turn off that fire alarm and soon, she was going to get stabby. The endless blaring was enough to make a person plain nuts. She looked around for Elijah or the principal or someone to tell her what was going on while simultaneously trying to huddle deeper into her coat. She wished she'd thought to grab her knitted wool hat too. Her scalp was frozen solid, or at least it felt like it.

Through the swirling flakes, she spotted Elijah hurrying their way with...was that Chief Anderson next to him? Was it really a fire then? She'd almost had herself convinced that it was just a student prank since no one had been able to spot flames or smoke, but if the fire chief was here...

That wasn't a good sign, for sure. Worried, she yelled over the din of the alarms, "Is there a fire, then?"

"We don't know," Anderson yelled back. "I've got a crew on its—"

Two sirens added to the cacophony and Hannah clapped her hands over her ears. "Mylanta, this noise is going to drive me nuts!" she yelled at the top of her lungs. She didn't even know who she was yelling at. She only knew that she was a hairbreadths away from losing it completely.

Two fire trucks squealed to a stop in front of the school; the sirens mercifully dying away even as the lights kept flashing. Men in full turnout gear poured out of the trucks but through the hazy snow, Hannah couldn't tell who was who. She knew everyone on the fire crew, of course – in a town this size, it'd be impossible not to – but that didn't mean she'd recognize them through biting snow tearing at her skin and eyes.

"While they're searching the school for the fire," the new fire chief shouted over the noise, "Elijah here says that his daughter Brooklyn is missing, and that you're her teacher. Have you seen her since lunch?"

She shook her head frantically. "I was just starting to do my after-lunch check of the students when the fire alarm went off. Her friends said that she went to the library to turn in a book but no one's seen her since."

"My guys are going to do a sweep of the school so we can figure out if there's really a fire or not – if someone just pulled the alarm to cause problems, we shouldn't be having the students stand outside in this weather. They'll keep their eyes peeled for Brooklyn while they're clearing out the school. They'll radio me if they find her. In the meanwhile, we need to call her mother and see if she knows anything. Maybe Brooklyn walked home without permission and her mom doesn't know we're looking for her."

Hannah just nodded, keeping her thoughts to herself. If Brooklyn was going to run away, she wouldn't be running away to her mother's house. Brooklyn's plea rang in Hannah's ears.

*You don't never get drunk.*

No, Brooklyn was definitely not running away to her mother's house.

"Elijah, what's your ex-wife's number?" the fire chief asked as he dug his cell phone out of his pocket.

Elijah rattled the number off without blinking an eyelash, while Hannah silently counted her lucky stars that she wasn't the one calling that woman. She needed to stop being such a wimp, she knew she did, but still…

She couldn't help being grateful to the tips of her frozen toes that she wasn't having to tell the hateful drunk that her daughter was missing.

"Sarah Morland?" the fire chief said when Sarah answered. "This is Fire Chief Anderson here in Sawyer. I'm afraid I have bad news. A fire alarm has gone off here at the elementary school, and in the chaos afterwards, no one has been able to locate your daughter. Have you seen or heard from Brooklyn since she left for school this morning?"

"I'm ssoooorrrryyyyyyyy…" Patrick wailed. "He made me swear that I wouldn't tell nobody."

Hannah jerked her gaze away from the fire chief to look down at her student, completely perplexed. "Patrick, what are you talking about?" she yelled over the fire alarm that was still. going. off. and. was. never. going. to. stop. and. was. going. to. drive. her. absolutely. insane. in. about. ten. seconds. or. so.

"Are you being serious right now?" the fire chief demanded, sounding pissed. Hannah jerked her head back up to look at him. Why was he so angry?

"Dayton made me make a blood oath I wouldn't tell!" Patrick sobbed, yanking her attention back towards him. She felt a little nauseous, like she'd been plopped smack down in the middle of a tennis match.

"I'm going to be contacting the police chief over this," the fire chief shouted into the phone. "Your reckless actions could very well have led to one of my men getting hurt, or these children getting ill from standing out in this weather." He shoved his phone back into his pocket, looking livid. "Sarah picked Brooklyn up from school," he said disgustedly. "Claims she forgot to check her out of the office. They're on their way to Boise to go *grocery* shopping." He seemed incredulous at the idea of a student missing school to go grocery shopping, but Hannah wasn't surprised. Parents routinely took their kids out of school for the skimpiest of reasons. "She sounds sauced. Is she a drinker?" he demanded of Elijah.

Elijah nodded, the panic stamped all over his face melting away a bit at the news that at least his daughter hadn't been kidnapped by some sicko.

*Although being in a vehicle with a drunk and nasty mother isn't much better.*

Hannah really wasn't sure what to feel about this news.

"He's going to be mad at me," Patrick announced as he tugged on her coat sleeve. "But I had to tell."

Hannah looked back down at her student, struggling to keep up with everything happening around her. Brooklyn had been kidnapped by her drunk mother, the fire alarm from Hades was still going off, she was freezing to death in a blizzard that only penguins in Antarctica could appreciate, and Patrick was...

*What was Patrick talking about?*

"Who's going to be mad at you?" she shouted over the noise as Chief Anderson left to tell the principal that the search was off for Brooklyn, at least. He was radioing it out to his guys as he hurried through the whipping snow.

"Dayton!" Patrick shouted impatiently. "He's the one who pulled the fire alarm. He didn't want to take the spelling test this afternoon. He's hiding in the boy's bathroom now. I can't get him to come out. He's gonna be real mad at me for telling you."

Hannah wasn't sure if she should laugh or cry or drop into a heap on the frozen ground and beat it with her fists. *Teachers deserve hazard pay. Truly, I don't think live enemy fire could be worse than this.*

A part of her felt guilty for not noticing his absence earlier, but he'd come into class as lunch was ending, and in the craziness of it all, she hadn't thought to check for him a second time. After she'd discovered Brooklyn was missing, everything else flew straight out of her brain.

She looked up at Elijah. "Tell the principal that it was Dayton who pulled the fire alarm," she said calmly, "and that there is no fire. Patrick, you come with me. Mrs. Damerell," she called out to the elderly librarian, "I need you to take my class back inside when the alarm stops and the principal gives us the all clear." She was one of the few adults around who didn't have classes of their own that they were responsible for, so Hannah didn't feel bad about dumping her class off onto the elderly woman's shoulders. She turned to her class and shouted, "You guys listen to Mrs. Damerell and be good when you get back into the classroom. I'll be there in a minute."

Her hand clamped down on Patrick's shoulder and she started heading towards the warmth of the school, dragging him along with her. "Which bathroom is he in?" she hollered over the alarm. Mr. Zeller was no doubt on his way to turn the thing off, and Hannah could only mentally beg him to hurry. "The one closest to us or the one on the other end?"

Blessed silence dropped over the school just as Hannah opened the front doors, dragging an unhappy Patrick along behind her. It was almost painful not to have the fire alarm going off; it was still ringing faintly in her ears. She wanted to weep from happiness anyway. If she never heard another fire alarm in her life, it would be too soon.

"This end," Patrick said glumly, clearly not happy about being included in this expedition to find Dayton. "He's gonna be real mad at me for telling," he said mournfully. "Do I *have* to come with you?"

Hannah made a beeline for the boy's bathroom, her hand

clamped on his shoulder, not giving an inch. "Patrick, they have video cameras trained on every single fire alarm in the school. If Dayton pulled the alarm, the principal has it on videotape. Dayton isn't getting into trouble because of you. He was going to be in trouble no matter what. I'm just able to find him faster because of you."

"Oh."

Hannah wanted to shake his thin, bony shoulders. Ten-year-old boys were sure idiotic sometimes.

She paused at the doorway of the bathroom. "Dayton, are you in here?" she called out. She heard some shuffling noises but no response. "Dayton, I know you pulled the fire alarm. You need to come out now."

One of the stalls burst open and Dayton came tumbling out. "How did you know I—" He spotted Patrick and jerked to a stop. "You told her!" he yelled accusingly. Patrick shrunk down behind his teacher, using her body as a defensive shield against his friend. "I'm gonna whoop your ass—"

"Dayton Meier!" Hannah hollered, and Dayton shut up and looked at her, defiantly scared to death. "As I was just explaining to Patrick here," she said in her best icy, you-are-in-deep-trouble-mister voice, "there are video cameras trained on every single fire alarm in the school. There's no way you could pull one without it being caught on tape. So, don't get upset with Patrick; he was worried that your classmates were all going to freeze to death in the blizzard you sent them out into, and wanted them to be able to come back inside."

Patrick hadn't technically told her that, but she was sure that was his reasoning. And if it wasn't, well, it should've been.

"A blizzard?" Dayton repeated, even quieter this time. He'd veered firmly into Terrified Land as he realized the full extent of what he'd done.

"Yeah, a full-blown blizzard. Started while all of your classmates were standing out in it, trying to be safe from a fire that does not exist," she said sarcastically, wanting to shake some sense into him. "Not everyone had time to grab their jacket and gloves before heading outside. You probably caused more than a few of the students in this school to get very, very sick from being out in that without proper clothing on. This is as serious as it gets, Dayton, and all because you didn't want to take a test." She shook her head in dismay. "C'mon, you and Patrick are heading down to the principal's office. He'll take care of you from there."

As she directed the dejected pair towards the front office, the thought she'd had back at the beginning of the school year, all those months ago, popped into her mind: *If Dayton is anything like his older brother, this is going to be an interesting school year.*

Well, she certainly got that part right.

# CHAPTER 31

## ELIJAH

APRIL, 2019

"Your Honor," Elijah said pleadingly, "I know she hasn't ever taken a breathalyzer test that she's failed. But there have been many times when I've called her and she was flat-out drunk in the middle of the afternoon. She was always a drinker when we were married, but she's gotten a whole lot worse since—"

"Mr. Morland," Judge Schmidt said crisply, "last time I checked, your ears are not a valid alcohol testing device recognized by the State of Idaho, and even if they were, there is no law against someone drinking in the confines of their own home."

"But—" Elijah jumped in, and the judge held up his hand, snapping, "Mr. Morland!" Elijah shut up. "You claim that she was drinking when she drove Brooklyn to Boise to go shopping. Again, your ears are not a valid alcohol testing device! She was properly repentant about causing worry and alarm that day when she forgot to check Brooklyn out of school; I am not about to take a daughter away from her mother for one simple, minor mistake. Children should be with their mothers whenever possible; it is best for the health of the child. Now, do not come before this court again and waste my time unless you have something to actually report. Good day!" He banged his gavel down with all his might, clearly wishing he could bring it down on Elijah's head instead. "Bailiff, who's next?" he snapped.

Sarah stood up, the most smug smile he'd ever seen on the face of a human being plastered all over her as she dragged Brooksy down the middle aisle after her and outta the courthouse. Her three lawyers in their fancy suits followed, not looking at him at all as they went past.

Mechanically, Elijah stood up, no lawyer on his side to follow him outta the courthouse. Lawyers cost money, and that was something he just didn't have enough of.

He stumbled out into the weak spring sunshine, the mountains making a valiant effort to beat back the snow, and forced back the urge to beat something of his own with his fists. Sarah's brand-new Escalade, maybe, or the smugness off her face, or the side of the courthouse building. Hell, maybe he could punch and beat and kick it until justice actually came outta it. He'd never liked Judge Schmidt much, but after hearing Hannah's story 'bout his son, Eli found it hard to even look the man in the eye.

*Do you know what kind of monster you raised?*

And the judge's belief that children should always be with their mommas unless they were proven criminals sure as shit didn't make him love the man any more.

*My money is good enough for Sarah to spend on my daughter; sure seems like I oughta be good enough to see my daughter more than once every two weeks.*

Well, of course he saw her more than that, but that was only 'cause he was willing to clean up puddles of piss and puke and scrub windows 'til they shined. The court wasn't any help in making it happen, that was for damn sure.

He drove over to Hannah's house, carefully parking in back so no one could see him go in, and slipped inside. He hated doing it that way – he hated not being able to walk through the front door like any other person could, like he wasn't good enough for Hannah either. It'd been rubbing on him for months now, but after the trouncing he'd just received in court…

He was all twisted up with anger. He could feel it bouncing around inside of him, pushing at him, making him wanna swing and hit something to let some of it out.

"How did it…" Hannah came out of the kitchen and caught sight of his face, and stopped mid-sentence. "That bad?" she asked softly, hurrying to his side so she could run her hand up and down his arm.

He felt the tiniest bit of anger disappear at her touch. Just a little, but still…Being around her was good for his soul.

He shook his head in disgust. "Judge Schmidt is a low-down snake. I'm worth a bucket of warm spit 'cause I'm a guy, but boy howdy, my money sure is good enough for Sarah." He wanted to rip at the world – stomp it into pieces like his own world was stomped into pieces. Was he ever gonna win against his ex? It sure didn't feel like he would. Why keep trying? What was the point?

Hannah wrapped her arms around him and snuggled up against his chest. "I know Judge Schmidt doesn't see it," her voice caught just a bit on the name 'Schmidt' but she kept going and he only knew it'd happened 'cause he knew her well enough to hear the little things, "but everyone who knows you and Sarah both, also knows that you are by far the better parent. I've never met a father who loved his child as much as you do, and I'm an elementary school teacher. I've met a lot of fathers."

He laughed a little at that. Leave it up to Hannah to make him smile even when he was angry enough to spit nails. She had a true talent.

His smile quickly faded away, though, as reality seeped back in. "I'm just frustrated 'cause I'm going in circles. I'm 31 years old, and I have no career. No schooling past high school. My marriage was a disaster, and all my ex does now is work hard to keep me from seeing my own daughter, and seeing how drunk she can get before noon each day. I have to wipe up yellow piss off the floor as a job. I'm renting this piece-of-shit house that looks like more than a few drug deals were done in it, and what do I have to show for all of this? I'm barely scraping by each month. I'm not good enough for you, Hannah. If I was a better man, I'd walk away. I already tried that once, though, and it turns out I don't have the self control to stay away."

He was snuggling her against him, running his hands up and down her back and through the prettiest hair he ever did see, glinting a golden red in the spring sunlight coming through the windows.

"I'm sorry I'm not a better man," he murmured. "I don't wanna walk away. I wanna marry you." He felt her stiffen just a bit in his arms, her breath disappearing as she stood there carefully, almost like she was afraid that if she moved, he'd change his mind. He laughed sadly. "Hannah, I've never met a sweeter, smarter, or prettier woman than you. If I didn't wanna marry you, you should check to make sure I'm not braindead or something. But you deserve so much more than me—"

"Elijah Morland," she scolded him, pulling back just a little out of his arms so she could glare up at him, "if I'm so amazingly smart, then don't you think I should know for myself if I want to marry you or not? You're saying I'm too smart for you, *and* that I'm too stupid to know that I'm too smart for you. I think that's a real trick."

He gaped down at her. "Shit," he groaned, "I didn't mean it that way. I just…haven't you heard the way I talk? And I never even went to community college, let alone got a real degree like you. I worked at Mr. Petrol's for years and years as their night manager 'cause then I could watch Brooksy during the day while Sarah went to work, but you know why else I worked there? 'Cause I couldn't find anything else. I divorced Sarah just about a year before I started at the school. I searched for a job high and low for that whole year, and found nothing until the janitor job came up. Turns out, all I'm good for is to scrub up some pee, and then give almost every last penny I make to my money-hungry bitch of an ex-wife. Excuse my French," he said quickly, feeling terrible for saying such a word around Hannah. It was the most accurate way to describe Sarah, but that didn't mean Hannah should be hearing that language.

Hannah narrowed her eyes at him. "We're not going to get sidetracked into your swearing habits," she announced. "Tell me, if you could pick any job in the world to do, what would it be?"

He shifted from foot to foot uncomfortably. This seemed suspiciously like she was thinking he was capable of doing any job in the world, and that just wasn't true. How was it that they'd been dating all of these months, and she was still this ignorant about him? Maybe that's why she hadn't broken up with him yet – she was too sweet and naïve to see the real him. What if he finally made her realize the truth, and so she walked away?

The thought was a stab to the gut.

"I don't know what you're thinking about," Hannah broke in, "but I want you to forget all of that for a minute. Forget me, forget Sarah, forget Brooklyn, forget where you live or what your parents think about you. What do you want to do as a job? What do you like to do?"

He shut his eyes tightly, trying to focus on what she was asking. Maybe if he wasn't looking at her while he thought, he could think clearer. "I like to do things with my hands," he said slowly. "I like figuring things out. Things make a certain sense to me, whereas words…I don't know how to say 'em or spell 'em or what they mean—"

"We're focusing on what you're *good* at," she told him bluntly. "Forget all of that. Now, you like to figure things out because they make sense to you – what kind of things?"

"Carpentry, vehicles, light fixtures – *things*. Where I can see it and move it around with my hands, not on some computer or something."

"Hmmm…Maybe we ought to have you go to an employment center where you can be tested for your various aptitudes," she said seriously, as if that was supposed to mean a damn thing to him. At his blank stare, she clarified, "Where they help you figure out what you're good at."

He almost said, "Not big words, obviously," but didn't. Some things were too true to be funny.

"We'll figure it out," she said softly. "Together, we'll figure it out."

*We.*

It was turning out to be his favorite word of all. Short, simple – even he knew how to spell it and say it – and most of all, it meant him and Hannah together.

Yup, that was a word he liked.

# CHAPTER 32

## HANNAH

"Hannah, the principal wants you to come to his office after school," Mrs. Worsop said when Hannah answered the phone, trying to juggle it and papers she was grading and the banana that constituted her lunch that day.

The banana paused halfway to her mouth.

"Yeah?" Her voice squeaked on the word, as if she was a 14-year-old boy going through puberty. She cleared her throat, trying to push down the panic those simple words wrought in her. "Umm…Do you know why?"

"He didn't say, but he did tell me that it wasn't optional." The secretary lowered her voice and said conspiratorially, "He looked upset to me, Hannah. I don't think it's good."

"Okay," she said faintly, and hung up the phone. The world whooshed in and out of focus around her as she scrambled to come up with what he could possibly want to talk to her about. The end of school was just ten days away. She'd already signed her contract for the next school year. He couldn't be upset about her teaching style or the way this year had gone if he'd offered her a contract for next year, right? And, if he was going to be upset by how she taught, why, certainly he would've said something to her in the past twelve years about it.

She wanted nothing more than to crawl under her desk and hide for the rest of the afternoon, but of course that wasn't possible. Her students were pretty well behaved – even Dayton had calmed down after the fire alarm incident, his parents finally believing that his behavior was something to take notice of and were acting accordingly – but there were limits, even for them. If she didn't make an appearance for an entire afternoon, they'd certainly start to notice something was wrong, and her students calling the office, looking for her, wouldn't exactly help this meeting along after school.

*Wouldn't that just make a fine impression on Mr. Zeller.*

She looked down at her banana, her stomach turned by the idea of eating anything at all, and pitched it into the trash can. This was going to be one horribly long afternoon. A classroom full of students just dying to start their summer break, combined with the impending doom of a one-on-one meeting with a pissed-off principal.

She longed to find Elijah to have him hold her and stroke her hair and tell her that everything was going to be okay, but of course, that wasn't an option at school. They were nothing but professional colleagues on the Cleveland Elementary School grounds. The few times they'd had to pretend in front of other teachers – Amelia not being counted in that group since she already knew – Hannah had been sure that the sparks flying between them were enough to set the school roof on fire, but no one had ever said a word to them, so maybe it wasn't as obvious as the blood in her face felt it was, blushing being an Olympic sport for her at this point.

The students filed in after lunch, and as Hannah plastered

on her best and most cheerful smile as she looked out over her students, she wondered anew why Brooklyn had been gone from school that day. She hadn't come in early to get cleaned up, and Juan and Juniper had just shrugged when she'd asked them where she was at. Was she sick? Surely Sarah would've told Elijah if she was, but Elijah had been just as clueless as Hannah when she'd asked him out in the hallway right before lunch.

Was that it? Them talking in the hallway about Brooksy being gone from school today? Surely not. She'd talk to any parent on that topic. As a teacher, talking to a parent about a student missing school was practically mandatory. And she'd been such a good girl during the conversation. Not once did she run her fingers through his hair to straighten its mussy waves, or across his cheek to help stroke the stress inside of him away. It'd been difficult to keep her hands to herself; he looked like he was wearing a 100-lb pack on his shoulders all the time, and it was hard for her not to want to take some of that onto herself.

"Miss Lambert?" Tahlia said hesitantly, yanking her back to the present to find 25 pairs of eyes all staring at her.

Her face flushed red. Again. Not just an Olympic sport at this point, she was going to win the freaking gold medal for it.

"Sorry, class, just thinking about everything we have to do this afternoon. Lots of projects to finish up before I let you loose for the summer, of course." She sounded cheerful and on top of things and organized, all traits that were normally true but today? Today she was just faking every bit of it.

At 3:12, she knocked on the open door of Principal Zeller's office. "Mr. Zeller?" she said, peering around the corner, trying not to throw up from the nerves pushing their way up her throat. She liked her principal, as much as she could like any male adult who was also her boss, which was probably the only reason she wasn't fainting dead away on the floor from pure petrification.

"Hello, Miss Lambert, come in," he said, pushing away from his desk and leaning over it to shake her hand before saying, "Close the door behind you and take a seat."

*Close the door?* This was getting worse by the moment. The edges of her vision darkened as the room tunneled, and she realized that either she needed to start breathing, or she really would pass out on the floor.

*Breathe in, breathe out. Breathe in —*

"Do you know why I've asked you in here, Miss Lambert?" he asked, pulling her gaze back to him.

She shook her head, trying to focus on his face. His wrinkles and gray hair were swooshing in and out of focus and she wished most desperately in that moment for her glasses to be back on her face. They'd make focusing easier, plus they'd be a shield—

"No, I don't know," she forced herself to say. Okay, more like whisper, but who was counting?

"I got a phone call from Ms. Morland today – first thing this morning. I know that after that whole fire alarm debacle, she's no one's favorite person, but she was hot to trot on the phone. Accusing you of all sorts of things. Is it true that you've been taking care of Brooklyn every morning?"

Hannah's heart, which had come to a complete stop at the words "Ms. Morland" began thumping along slowly, painfully, as she scrambled to figure out what she was in trouble for. Not her relationship with Elijah, but her relationship with Brooklyn?

It'd been so long since she'd started "taking care of Brooklyn every morning," as the principal put it, that she'd almost forgotten that she wasn't supposed to be.

"Yes, sir," she whispered, and then straightened in her chair. "Brooklyn was coming to school without being bathed; her mother hadn't combed her hair or made her brush her teeth in ages. The kids started teasing her at recess, singing, 'Brooklyn needs a bath' and calling her Stinky Brooksy. So I started helping her get ready in the morning."

The principal cocked an eyebrow at her. "Is it true that you lied to her mother in order to get Brooklyn here to school early so you could do this?"

"Yes, sir," she whispered, squirming in her chair. "I told Sarah that Brooklyn needed extra tutoring with her math, so Sarah was to bring in her daughter early each day."

"And did she need help with her math?" the principal asked. He sounded like a lawyer in a courtroom, grilling the defendant.

And oh, how she felt like a criminal. She, the most pacifist, easygoing, law-abiding citizen on the planet, had somehow turned criminal when she hadn't been looking.

"No, sir. Although," she added quickly, "we would work on her multiplication facts while I was brushing her hair or washing her face. We'd drill until she could multiply, divide, add, or subtract all in her head in the blink of an—"

"Miss Lambert!" the principal snapped. Hannah shut up. "I appreciate your efforts, truly I do, but it is not your place to be Brooklyn's mother. She has a mother, and at the moment, she's one truly pissed-off mother who wants to make a whole lot of waves. She's threatening to go to the school board with this."

The world sort of disappeared in that moment. She had her eyes open but she couldn't see anything and she couldn't hear anything and she felt herself slumping sideways like a doll propped up wrong and almost without meaning to, her head dropped between her knees and she gasped for air, trying to hear or think or…or something.

She felt the principal's hand on her shoulder – at least she assumed it was he, unless someone else had come into the office – and a low rumble of words, but they weren't making sense.

*Breathe in, breathe out.*

Slowly, the cottony cocoon that had wrapped itself around her began to fade away and she could hear words again. "Hannah, can you hear me? Nod if you can hear me."

Her head still tucked firmly between her legs, she nodded just slightly.

"Oh thank God," the principal said heavily. "I thought I was going to have to call an ambulance or something. Can you sit up?"

She forced herself upright, clinging to the armrests of her chair with all of her might. She smiled wanly at the principal, who'd made his way back to his side of the desk. "Sorry, sir, I don't know what happened—" She drew in a deep breath, still feeling faint. "What happened there," she finished weakly.

"We haven't even gotten to the bad part yet," the principal warned her.

"We…we haven't?" Hannah echoed. What could possibly be worse than being dragged before the school board to account for her sins?

"Ms. Morland also claims that you've been having an affair with her ex-husband, but I told her absolutely—" He broke off and stared at her. "No, Hannah, you haven't. Tell me you haven't."

She just sat there, frozen.

"Miss Lambert, how could you?!" He looked positively shocked to his core, like she just announced she'd taken up pole-dancing on the weekends down at the titty bar. "He's your coworker and the father of a student. What made you think that was a good idea?!" He was practically shouting at this point and she began to wish for the school board instead. The chances were that they wouldn't actually shout at her.

Maybe.

"I don't know," she said truthfully. "It just sort of… happened."

The principal was veering dangerously between pissed off and disbelieving. She wasn't sure where he would land, and more importantly, where she wanted him to land. There was really no good ending to this discussion that she could see.

"I cannot tell you who you can date in your free time, unless it interferes with your job here at the school. So, with that in mind, Elijah Morland is the last man on the planet who you should be dating."

Funny he would say that. She'd had exactly the same thought herself all those months ago. And then…well, it had started to seem like a good idea.

A really good idea.

"I know, sir," she whispered, staring down at her hands twisting away in her lap.

"The only thing saving you right now," Mr. Zeller said heavily, "is that you're one of the best teachers at this school. If I could somehow gift other teachers here with half the heart you have, this would be a much better school. I don't want to fire you, honestly I don't, but out of all of the stunts to pull, this was a real doozy."

*Fire. I could be fired.*

This was suddenly going much, much worse than she'd imagined it could.

What was that called – a failure of imagination? That was what she had.

Getting yelled at by the school board was sounding better by the moment, if it meant she still had a job when it was all over. What would she do if she couldn't be a teacher anymore? Teaching was what she was meant to be. It was who she was. It was all she'd ever wanted to do. Her father loved to tell stories about her lining up dolls in rows when she was just a toddler and teaching them to sing the ABCs.

Back when her father could remember who she was, of course, or what she did as a toddler.

"The only way forward out of this disaster," the principal announced, "is to fire Elijah, put you on a year's probation, and put extra restrictions in place in regards to reporting back to me about students' welfare. I'm going to trust that after this little stunt with Elijah, you're not going to start dating Mr. Pettengill, correct?" The sarcasm was practically dripping off his tongue.

"No, sir!" she gasped. Dating Mr. Pettengill…she'd rather be fired a hundred times over. "But…Elijah needs this job. It's how he sees Brooklyn—"

"This is the best I can do," Mr. Zeller said crisply, "and more than you deserve under the circumstances, considering just this year's behavior. But when I look at the past twelve years of your work here…" His face softened. "You really have been an exemplar employee, Hannah. I don't wish you ill. I just think that this little escapade wasn't your shining moment, and Ms. Morland is about to make everyone's life miserable because of it, mine included. I can't say that I'm real excited about that prospect. Between you, me, and the fencepost, her inheriting all of that money from her parents' death was the worst thing that could've ever happened to her. She has a lot more money than she does kindness or empathy, and that's not a healthy combination. But it all boils down to the fact that she can hire enough lawyers to keep our school district hopping for the next year, and we just do not have the money to fight off a protracted lawsuit. I proposed this solution to the board, and they agreed to it, but there is no wiggle room here. Do you have any questions?"

She shook her head numbly. *Stupid, stupid, stupid Hannah. You try putting your toe out of line the one time in your whole life, and you get a good man fired, you get a child into trouble, and you get your employer sued by a money-hungry woman who wants nothing more than to make everyone's life miserable.*

*When you screw up, you sure do a bang-up job of it.*

Her head snapped up. "Hold on, what's happening with Brooklyn?" she asked pleadingly. Yeah, she *was* getting a child into trouble. What had Sarah done to Brooklyn when she'd found out? Hannah had visions of Brooklyn being locked in a dank, windowless basement without food or water. She felt ill. "Is she in trouble with her mother? Is this why she wasn't at school today?"

Of *course* this was why she hadn't been at school that day;

even as the words left her mouth, she felt stupid saying them. She was ten miles behind everyone else, trying to play catch up to the world around her.

"Ms. Morland noticed a pink barrette in her hair and asked her where it came from. According to Ms. Morland, you'd told her daughter to lie to her." Hannah opened up her mouth to defend herself and the principal held up his hand. "Don't tell me; I don't want to know. After she finally got Brooklyn to tell her the truth, she's been grounded ever since, according to her mother. She won't be coming back to school this year; with only a week left in the school year, it's much too late to move her to a different teacher, and as Ms. Morland informed me this morning, she'd rather 'eat broken glass' than have her daughter taught by you any longer. You need to calculate her grades based on the work done thus far; do not include any project she isn't able to finish. Any other questions?"

She shook her head numbly.

"Good. I'll draw up formal papers in regards to what happened here, and after you read them over and sign them, they'll be put into your official record."

She nodded her head again. Official record. This would haunt her for the rest of her career.

She swallowed down hard on the bile rising up in her throat.

"You're a good teacher, Hannah," the principal said softly as she rose to wobbly feet. "You just need to remember where the line is, and stay on this side of it."

She nodded numbly yet again, feeling like one of those bobble-head dolls people put on the dashboard of their vehicles, and escaped out of the principal's office before he could see the tears trailing hot and painful down her cheeks. She avoided the gaze of Mrs. Worsop as she hurried past and down to her classroom. Putting her head down on her desk, she let a few deep, wrenching sobs escape.

But before she could really get into a good cry, though, she forced herself to her feet and snagged her purse and jacket. She was going to go home and spend some time with her horses. Nothing made her feel better than a long ride on Wildflower... except a long hug from Elijah, of course.

But that was over now. Over, and would never be coming back again.

# CHAPTER 33
## ELIJAH

BACON THE HAMSTER – he'd barely been able to talk Brooklyn out of calling it Ham the Hamster – stared back at Elijah with one beady eye.

"I'm fired, Bacon. For the first time in my life, my employer said I'm not good enough for 'em and they don't want me back ever again. Fired. Not," he raised a finger and shook it at the hamster, "that I was in love with the job or something. Who could be in love with cleaning up piss and scraping up gum and wiping up puke? Nobody, that's who. But it's the principle of the matter."

He took another swig straight outta the whiskey bottle, hardly even feeling the burn anymore. He wasn't normally much of a drinker, but since his ex drank like a fish and got everything she wanted outta life, he figured that he'd try it, too. At this point, it sure as hell couldn't hurt.

It wasn't like he had a job to get up for the next morning, or a kid to watch over.

"Nope, I have nothing at all," he told Bacon. Bacon, apparently not as interested in this conversation as he really ought to have been, wandered off and started eating his pellets. "Eat slow," he called out at the back of Bacon's head. "I don't know when I'll be able to buy another bag for you. You best enjoy it while you can."

Bacon didn't so much as twitch an ear at him.

Elijah slunk down in the kitchen chair, staring blearily at the bottle in his hand. Was it almost gone? He wasn't sure. He held it up to the light and stared through the dark bottle.

A bit swished around in the bottom, but nothing more.

"Dammit all, I can't even get good 'n drunk without running outta alcohol. Just who in the hell did I piss off in a former life?"

Bacon moved from the food bowl over to the wheel and began running in endless circles.

"See? That's why I bought Brooklyn a hamster. 'Cause your life is just as pointless as mine." He shook the almost-empty whiskey bottle at the oversized rat and then changed his mind and cradled it up against his chest. If he wasn't careful, he might spill the last of it, and then where would he be?

His cell phone rang and he perked up, snagging it with fumbling fingers off the counter. Maybe it was Hannah, finally calling him ba—

*Aaron Morland* was flashing up on the screen. Elijah dropped the phone back down to the counter with a sigh. He loved his brother, he surely did, but the last thing he wanted in that moment was to listen to a lecture about how he screwed this all up. He already knew that and didn't need a know-it-all older brother to rub his face in it.

He took the last swig of the alcohol in the bottle, even tipping it up and running his tongue around the edge, and then hucked it towards the kitchen trash. It clanked and smashed its way into place, finally stopping its noise and leaving him in peace.

"You sure are a dumbass," he said to his all-too-empty kitchen. "Your father told you that you were, and you thought you'd prove him wrong, but you didn't. You proved that no matter how hard you try, you aren't ever gonna be worth anything, and don't you never, ever forget it again."

He swung his hand down with a satisfying smash onto his piece-of-shit kitchen table he'd rescued off the side of the road years ago, and watched it fall to jagged pieces onto the floor, destroyed forever.

Destroyed, just like his damn life.

# CHAPTER 34

## HANNAH

"HEY, DADDY," Hannah said softly, stroking his liver-spotted hand. She used to love his hands – so big and strong, they could take on the world. Now they were gnarled and bony and thin, with dark spots telling the world his age, if they didn't catch it from his face or stooped shoulders.

He peered up at her for just a moment, and she could tell that he was trying to figure out who she was, and then his attention was caught by the children's puzzle in front of him and he looked back down at the table. "They sure make these things hard these days," he announced to the room as he tried to slot a piece into place and failed. "Why, when I was a kid, they were a whole lot easier to put together."

He'd put this one together dozens of times, each time slower than the last, but Hannah didn't tell him that. At least he wasn't giving up on it like he'd given up on door locks.

"Who did you say you are?" he demanded as he pushed on another piece, trying to force it into place.

"I'm Hannah Lambert," she said, not bothering to explain to him that she was his daughter. Again. They'd done that bit so many times in the past, she could almost recite every line by heart. Just about the time she'd finally get him convinced that she really was his daughter, his mind would slip away and he'd forget it all.

Talking to him was like talking to a black hole – one that made sometimes appropriate, but mostly inappropriate, comments back. Therapists and lawyers and doctors swore oaths that they would never reveal a patient's information without their consent, but telling Theodore Lambert? It was a rock-solid guarantee.

It was impossible to repeat something you don't remember hearing, and ten minutes from now, he wouldn't remember any of this. No chance of information leaking out of him.

She picked up a piece of the puzzle showing orange oak leaves against the fall sky, and tried to push it into place, failing just as badly as her father. She'd never been very good at puzzles. "I met a guy, Daddy. His name is Elijah Morland. He has a daughter named Brooklyn but he calls her Brooksy. She's his mini-me, and never have I seen a father love a daughter more than Elijah loves Brooklyn. Except you and me – you always loved me so much."

"I'm your...father?" he asked slowly, his watery blue eyes peering up at her through his bushy eyebrows.

"The one and only," she said with a painful laugh. She didn't feel like laughing. She swallowed the lump in her throat. "But Eli and I weren't supposed to date, Daddy, and we did anyway, and I screwed it all up, and I ruined his life. Now he's never going to get custody of his daughter – he doesn't even have a job. How is he supposed to take care of a child? And Brooklyn will grow up without her papa, and..."

The tears were rolling down her cheeks again. A small part of her was shocked to realize that she still had tears left in her. She would've thought she was all cried out.

Apparently not.

Her father patted her cheek. "It'll all work out, dear. Now..." His face clouded up. "What was your name again?"

"I'm Hannah Lambert," she whispered. "I better go. I'll see you later." She pressed a kiss to his wrinkled cheek and hurried out of the room, hearing him mutter, "They sure make these things hard these da—" as the door swung shut behind her.

She swiped at the tears trailing down her cheeks with the backs of her hands as she scurried past the front desk, avoiding eye contact with Ms. Blackburn, the head director of the center. Usually she like chatting with her, but not today. Not while her eyes were doing their best broken-faucet impersonation.

She checked the time on her phone as she slid into her car. Five minutes to get over to the Muffin Man for a meeting of the Early Spinster Club. Michelle had texted her and said that either she showed up at the bakery, or Carla and Michelle would show up on her front doorstep. Hannah had reluctantly agreed to come to the bakery. Since school had ended three days before, she hadn't left the house until today when she'd gone to visit her father.

Not that a visit to her father cheered her up, of course, although at this point, she wasn't sure what would cheer her up.

Hmmm…actually, she did. She wanted time to go back 15 days so she could live again in a world where she was happy and Elijah was her boyfriend and…

She was snuffling again, which was ridiculous. She refused to go into the bakery with her eyes all red and puffy. Michelle and Carla had already heard what had gone down through the grapevine that was Sawyer, Idaho, but she didn't need to confirm their worst suspicions. Bravely, she forced the tears away, wiping her cheeks clean and blowing her nose, and then, with her head held high, she marched through the bakery to slide into their regular booth.

With one wavery smile to the both of them, she burst into tears again.

*Way to keep a stiff upper lip, Hannah. Why, I bet they can hardly even tell you're upset.*

She was hiccuping. She hated hiccuping.

Carla pulled her against her generous chest, stroking Hannah's tear-soaked hair away from her face, while Michelle railed against the unfairness of it all, waving her arm around in the air like she was directing an orchestra only she could hear.

"You were just taking care of a little girl who needed the attention and love because her *alcoholic,*" Michelle hissed the dirty word, "mother was too drunk off her ass to do it herself. Did you tell the principal that you'd been taking care of this child for months and months now, and her darling, doting mother just barely noticed? Poor Brooklyn was basically raising herself. At ten years old! How dare you get into trouble for helping her become a beautiful young woman! You shoulda got a medal, not a year's probation!"

Michelle was thundering with all of the might and power of a Baptist preacher by time she was done, and Carla was right there, cheering her on. "Couldn't have said it better myself!" she shouted.

Hannah wanted to crawl under the booth and hide. She knew the entire town of Sawyer had heard what'd happened, but there was a difference between knowing that on an intellectual level versus discussing it openly in public.

Just when she didn't think she could get any more embarrassed, Sugar came around from behind the counter with a huge dog whistle of appreciation for Michelle's speech.

"You preach it, sister!" she practically hollered. "This town is ridiculous on the best of days, but what Sarah Morland and that *judge,*" she sneered the word, "have done is beyond that."

*Sugar. Mylanta, it's Sugar.*

Hannah wasn't surprised by the fact that Sugar was there. She was, after all, Gage's primary employee, and had worked at the bakery for years now. She'd waited on their little Early Spinster's Club meeting dozens of times over the years.

But today, Sugar was standing up for Hannah in a very public way, and honestly, she shouldn't. She didn't know she shouldn't, but Hannah knew, and the guilt of that truth was weighing her down.

Sugar was the wife of the new fire chief in town, but before she'd married him, she'd been married to Dickwad. In fact, she'd been forced into marriage to Dickwad after she'd been caught in the act with him on graduation night.

Hannah looked up at Sugar, her petite form right back to its pre-pregnancy curves like she hadn't just given birth two months before, and she gulped.

Hard.

*Guilt.*

*So. Much. Guilt.*

She'd wanted to apologize for years to Sugar for failing her by not reporting Dickwad to the authorities, or at least warned Sugar against dating him, but somehow, she'd never found a convenient time to do so.

She hadn't exactly been trying hard, to put it mildly.

"Uhh, Sugar, can you take a break?" Hannah asked her, her voice squeaking a little with nerves. "I need…to talk to you about something."

*Today is already downright awful. Might as well blow it to smithereens, right?*

"Sure," Sugar said with a confused look, but she didn't ask any questions. "Hey Gage, I'm gonna sit a spell!" she hollered over her shoulder, and then slid into the booth next to Michelle. "What's up?"

"I've never told any of you guys this, but I owe Sugar an apology, so," she drew in a deep breath, "all of you guys might as well hear it."

She had three pairs of curious eyes trained on her, which was scary as could be, but luckily it was just Carla, Michelle, and Sugar. They weren't scary.

Well, not unbearably scary.

She quickly recounted the details of her rape at the hands of Richard, trying not to delve too much into the gory details, mostly because she didn't want to think about them. She finished the story with the threat made by the then-15-year-old boy that if she told the police, he'd tell them that she'd been trying to seduce him for months and ruin her career before it'd even started.

"If I'd gone to the police anyway," she said miserably, "then you would've known not to date him, and you never would've been forced to marry him, and your life would be so much better. I let that happen to you by being a wimp and taking the easy way out. I'm so sorry, Sugar." She whispered the words that had been choking her throat for years on end.

If she'd been truly brave – as brave as she was supposed to be – she should've been able to shout them from the rooftop, but they were just so damn hard to say.

There was dead silence at the table for just a moment, and then Michelle burst out, "Ho-ly shit! I had no...I can't...I just... listen to me, I can't even talk! Me!" There was a short burst of laughter at that, because honestly, Michelle lacking for words just wasn't something that happened every day.

Hannah took a cautious peek up at Sugar, trying to ascertain how much Sugar hated her. Honestly, Hannah's fears and complete lack of courage in the face of difficulty had made Sugar's life a living hell for years on end.

So yeah, Sugar had every right to hate her guts and then some.

But instead, Sugar reached out and squeezed Hannah's hand, her chocolate brown eyes filling up with unshed tears.

"Oh, Hannah," she said softly. "I had no idea. I thought he'd just pushed his previous girlfriends to go farther than they'd wanted to go. I didn't know..." She shook her head. "And to think that man is still out wandering the streets, free as a jaybird. It's hard not to want to meet up with him in a dark alley, truly. I was afraid Jaxson would do just that after I told him what happened to me, but I think he realized that losing his two boys wasn't worth it." She shot Hannah a conspiratorial grin, wiping quickly at the tears that'd pooled at the corners of her eyes. "We have great taste, you and I. We picked the two men in Sawyer who'd do anything for their children, and they're better men for it. So, what are you and Elijah going to do now that he's been fired from the school?"

*What am I going to do? Mylanta, what* can *I do? It isn't like I have a choice in this or something.*

But they were all staring at her like the obvious truth needed to be spelled out for them, so, spell it out she did.

"Nothing," she said bluntly. "I can't keep dating him, obviously. I haven't even talked to him since the principal pulled me into his office; I'm too much of a wimp to return his phone calls. I just don't know what to say to him. 'Sorry I messed up your life. My bad!' Like…there is no entry in Miss Manner's book on this topic." She shot them a wry grin, but found they were just staring back at her, pity practically oozing out of the three of them.

"Hannah, you can't walk away from him," Michelle said bluntly, wading in first. No surprise there. "I've known you pert near all of our lives, and I've never seen you as happy as you were when you were with Elijah. I wouldn't have put the two of you together – you're just such opposites, you know?"

"I always thought you'd end up with an English professor or something," Carla put in, patting Hannah's hand loyally.

"But the heart is smart, and you two…you belong together," Michelle continued. "You love that little girl more than her own damn mother does. Elijah might be a little rough around the edges but he'd move heaven and earth for you, and he makes you happy."

"Cheerful," Carla added.

"Smiling all of the time," Sugar piped up.

"You can't let that go," Michelle announced with a finality of a woman who got what she wanted, when she wanted it. Hannah had figured out long ago that there was no telling

Michelle no. It would be like trying to hold back the tides of the ocean armed only with a tablespoon.

Hannah sank down in her seat, biting her lower lip as she stared back at her three friends. They made it seem so easy.

Just date him again, they said. It'll work out great, they said.

Except it'd put her career in jeopardy, and that was all she had left.

"I can't," she whispered. Michelle moved to protest, and Hannah held up her hand to stop her. Michelle subsided back into her seat, staring disbelievingly at Hannah. With every line in her body, it was obvious that she was simply waiting for Hannah to quit talking so she could set her straight. This just spurred Hannah on to talk faster so she could get it all out first.

"The principal…he was angry because Brooklyn was my student and sure, she isn't anymore, now that we're on summer break. And he was angry because Elijah was my co-worker and sure, he isn't anymore, now that the school district fired him. But I barely escaped that office with my job intact. My *career* intact. If I was fired from the school district, what would I do? Where would I work? I am a teacher. That's who I am, clear through my soul. I can't just go get a job down at the city filing paperwork or something. If I were to start dating Elijah again, I'd be thumbing my nose at the leadership of the school district. I'm already on thin ice with them; this would be their breaking point."

She sat back and realized with a painful bit of pride that she'd managed to shut them up. All three of them – even Michelle. Hannah wasn't much for arguing, so the temptation was strong to mentally pat herself on the back for actually winning an argument.

But on the other hand, this was one argument she didn't want to win. She wanted them to prove her wrong, somehow, some way. Come up with something she'd missed and fix all of her problems.

Sugar stood up first. "I'm sorry, Hannah, I have to go back to work. Gage is probably wondering what the hell happened to me. I wish I had something better to tell you. But, I will say this: My ex is one manipulative bastard, so don't feel one moment's guilt over not telling the world what happened at the city park. There was no way to win with that man – he made sure of it." She squeezed Hannah's shoulder consolingly on the way back to the kitchen.

Hannah looked at Michelle and Carla, her two closest friends in the world, and waited for them to say something. To wave a magic wand and fix her broken life.

Instead, Carla leaned over and wrapped her arm around Hannah's shoulders, pulling her close and stroking her hair. "Sorry, darlin'," she said into Hannah's hair. "Some days, life just sucks."

Truer words had never been spoken.

# CHAPTER 35

## ELIJAH

THE BUZZING of his cell phone on his nightstand pulled him up through the layers of sleep. Even in that world between asleep and awake, he was hoping and wishing and praying that it was Hannah calling him. Maybe she'd—

He forced one eyelid open and looked at his phone. *Aaron Morland,* the screen said. *3:22 a.m.*

Elijah sat straight up in bed. Why on God's green earth was Aaron calling him at 3:22 in the morning? Absolutely nothing good could come of this. Not a damn thing.

"Yeah?" he said gruffly, shoving the phone between his cheek and shoulder as he swung his legs outta bed. Whatever was going on, he needed to be dressed for it, and boxers and a t-shirt sure as shit didn't count.

"It's Brooklyn," Aaron said briskly. "Sarah was driving home from Boise stinking drunk and got in a car wreck just outside of town. Didn't make it over the Narrows, and the Escalade ended up at the bottom of the gorge. They're pulling Sarah out of it now, but the EMTs think they're gonna need the Jaws of Life to get Brooklyn out. You better come quick."

"Leaving. Going now. I'm—I'm on my way." He was

sputtering; his heart was racing so fast, he had a hard time breathing or thinking. *Brooksy. Brooksy. Bottom of the gorge. Brooksy.* "Are you out there already?" He could hear sirens in the background, and figured they were from his brother's police car.

"On my way myself. The sheriff, EMTs, and some of the city fire crew are already out there, working on the extraction. See you there." His brother hung up and Elijah stumbled around his bedroom, trying to get his brain and his body to match up.

Where was he going? What was he doing?

He'd always had a cool head in a crisis, but that was before Brooksy was involved in said crisis. Now, he found he could hardly decide which shoe to put on first.

He wanted to snatch his phone up and call Hannah and have her meet him out there; she'd wanna be out there if Brooksy was hurt, he just knew it. But he also knew that she didn't want anything to do with him. Over three weeks of deafening silence had made that perfectly clear.

He hurried out into the brisk June night air – it was only now hitting that time of the year when it didn't freeze overnight, although as cold as it felt right now, he was sure it was close.

As he slammed the gas pedal to the floor of his old truck, pushing it to go as fast as its big diesel engine would allow, he tried to remember back through everything Aaron had told him. He hadn't been real awake while Aaron'd been talking, and it was hard to remember now what he'd said.

*The Narrows. Shit. He said the Narrows.*

"C'mon, c'mon, c'mon you big piece of shit!" he yelled at his truck, his boot trying to push its way through the gas pedal and floorboards. The Narrows was a real narrow bridge on the road between Boise and Sawyer; probably built back in the 1800s or something, it was way too narrow for modern-day traffic. If a semi was driving from Boise to Sawyer, no oncoming traffic could be on the bridge at the same time 'cause there wasn't enough room. The county commissioners were always making noises about replacing it to make the drive to the big city safer, but shit like that cost money, and that was one thing Long Valley residents were always short on.

Thank God it wasn't too far of a drive from his house. The Narrows was right before you exited the mountains and the road opened into the Long Valley floor, giving you plenty of room on either side of the road. The ironic thing was, in less than a mile, Sarah woulda had to *try* to hit something. Brooksy woulda been safe.

And then the rest of what Aaron'd said really hit him.

Drunk.

Sarah had been driving drunk with Brooksy in the backseat.

"If you live through this, I swear to God, Sarah, I'm gonna kill you with my bare hands. If you've hurt one hair on Brooksy's head—" His hands were shaking as he tried to focus enough through the rage and fear inside of him to keep his own truck on the road. Running off the road and into a pine tree wouldn't help anyone.

In the darkness, he saw the flashing lights of the emergency vehicles long before he heard the wail of the sirens. His thoughts had become an endless repeat – *please God, please God, please God* – because there wasn't anything else he needed to add. God knew what to do from there.

He pulled off the road and into a ditch, slamming his truck into park and cutting the engine before taking off at a dead run towards the cluster of vehicles near the mouth of the bridge. Below the bridge was a real narrow and rocky gorge with plenty of rocks and pine trees to get impaled on, not to mention the river was running high with plenty of spring runoff to drown in.

*Please God, please God, please God—*

He saw Sheriff Connelly, his hat pushed back on his head as he talked to a group of men, and veered towards them. If he couldn't find Aaron right off the bat, Sheriff Connelly was his second choice. He'd been sheriff of the county for years, and he'd know just what to do.

"Where's my Brooksy?" Elijah roared, his fists pumping as he practically flew towards the group. "Is she all right?"

The sheriff reached out and grabbed Elijah before he could sprint past. "They got her out and are pulling her up now," he said calmly. "She's got a broken leg for sure; we don't know what else at this point – maybe some internal injuries. She's alive and she's breathing but she isn't conscious."

Elijah held himself together using every bit of self control that he knew he possessed, and some extra he didn't even know he had. "Sarah," he gasped around his lungs begging for air. He didn't do many sprints around the school with his mop bucket, and sadly enough, his little dash had left him struggling for breath. "How's she doing?"

"Alive and well," the sheriff said grimly. "People who're drunk usually fair better in a crash than the sober ones because they're so loose from being liquored up, they hardly get a scratch. She's being checked out by the EMTs and then I'll be taking her to the county jail. She blew a 1.4. Honestly, I think the injuries from the crash are gonna be the least of her worries. She might end up with alcohol poisoning."

"Good!" Elijah said bitterly. How had she even made it from Boise to here being that damn drunk? The legal limit was 0.8 for hell's sakes. "I can't believe…" He shook his head. There were a whole lot of things he couldn't believe, starting with the fact that the judge'd thought she was the better parent just 'cause she had a pair of tits on her. "Where's Brooksy being pulled up?"

The sheriff held up a cautionary hand. "I'll walk you over there but you gotta stay outta the way of the men working. You ain't gonna help your daughter by getting in their way. We clear?"

Elijah nodded his head begrudgingly. As hard as it was to

admit it, the sheriff was right. This was one time when someone else was the best person to take care of her.

*Unconscious…broken leg…internal injuries…*The godawful list went 'round and 'round in his head as he followed the sheriff through the darkness over to where floodlights had been set up, shining down into the steep rocky hillside below. *Please God, please God, please God…*

He heard the shouts of the men dimly, like someone had stuffed cotton into his ears and now he was wrapped up in the stuff. They were talking about how her blood pressure wasn't good, and they were trying to keep her neck still just in case she'd broken it, and all he could think was that he was real glad she wasn't awake for any of this. She would be terrified, strapped on her back to a board, being lifted up the side of a cliff in the dark, in pain and not knowing a soul around her…

*Please God, please God, please God…*

"Elijah!" He heard his name slurred through the darkness and knew without turning that it was Sarah yelling for his attention. He ignored her and kept focused on the scene below him, the careful lifting of a flat board through the darkness and shadows. If he went to Sarah's side right now, why, he might be tempted to wring her neck and then both of them would end up in jail. The last thing Brooksy needed right now was for the two of them to be idiots at the same damn time.

"Keep that woman away from me," he growled to the sheriff, "or I won't be responsible for my actions, so help me God."

"Can't say as I blame ya," the sheriff said quietly, and then turned to Officer Rios. "Shut her up," the sheriff barked. "I think she's caused enough problems for one night." The officer grabbed her arm and even through the darkness, Elijah caught the panic and fear on Sarah's face in the flash of the cop car lights as she was stuffed into the backseat, her hands cuffed behind her back.

"Elij—" The slammed door in her face cut her off.

Even as Elijah waited and prayed on the outside of the ring of men working to save his baby, he had to shake his head in wonder. Did Sarah honest to God think that he was gonna help her after she pert near killed their daughter? He knew she was self-centered, but that just plain took the cake.

Brooksy was getting closer to the top and Elijah was praying as hard as his soul would let him when he suddenly realized that he hadn't seen Aaron yet. "Where's my brother?" he asked the sheriff. "He called me and said he was on his way out here."

"He picked up a drunk driver on the way over," the sheriff said with a grim smile. "Damn idiots can't help themselves, I guess. He just radioed in that he's almost here."

"Okay, careful, careful, carry her this way," Chief Anderson said, carrying a floodlight and directing the men with the stretcher between them towards the ambulance.

"Why's the fire chief in charge of the EMTs?" Elijah asked, forcing himself not to rush to Brooksy's side. He'd promised the sheriff he wouldn't, and he wasn't about to do anything to hurt his little girl, even if that meant not taking care of her himself.

"He and the head of EMT swapped weekends to be on call. They thought it'd be a quiet weekend since the tourists haven't started pouring in yet and it ain't a holiday." He shot Eli a somber smile. "They were wrong, of course."

They began sliding Brooksy's small form into the ambulance, the flashing lights from every emergency vehicle lighting up the world in a bizarre pulsing disco light. "Elijah," the fire chief called out, turning on his heel and finding him through the darkness, "you wanna ride with her to the hospital?"

"Yes!" Elijah shouted, taking off at a dead run for the ambulance. He'd been forcing himself to hold back, and to finally be given permission to be there by her side – it was like someone had just told him he could breathe again. He scrambled into the back of the ambulance to find Jacob and Stu hunkered down beside her. They were both good guys that

Elijah knew from high school, and he could only thank God that they were the ones taking care of her.

"How is she?" he demanded. "Can I touch her?"

"Sure, sure, just don't knock any of the tubes out," Jacob said with a gentle smile. Elijah worked his way past the tubes and fluids to hold onto her tiny, soft hand. Her dirty blonde hair was real dirty tonight – caked so thick with dirt and mud and blood, it was hard to even tell where her hair was. If Hannah was here, she'd be clucking about cleaning her up.

He pushed the thought away. *Not now.*

"Her right leg is broken for sure," Stu said as the ambulance started forward over the uneven ground slowly, the siren wailing in the pre-dawn darkness. "Until we get her to the hospital, we won't know about anything internal. She could have a broken spine or internal bleeding and we wouldn't have a—"

"Stu," Jacob said, interrupting him. "No use telling Elijah every damn thing that could be wrong with her, when we just don't know."

"Right, right," Stu said, sending Elijah a tight smile. "She'll be fine, I'm sure." He didn't sound sure. "Kids heal fast," he added as an afterthought.

*Not from broken spines, they don't.*

Elijah squeezed Brooksy's hand. "You hear that?" he whispered, his voice breaking from the tears pushing their way up his throat. "Stu said you're gonna be fine, and he's an EMT, so he knows what he's talking about."

"Well—" Stu started, and Jacob shot him a dirty look.

"Stu, shut up," he said baldly.

Stu shut up.

Elijah ignored them both. He knew they were lying to him to make him feel better. He knew he was lying to Brooksy, on the off chance she could hear him, so he could make her feel better.

He knew all of that, and didn't give a rat's ass that pert near nothing that anyone was saying was true. His daughter was going through hell right now and if lying to her would make her one bit happier, he'd lie 'til he was blue in the face.

The ambulance sped up once it hit the smooth blacktop, but Elijah was still cursing under his breath at the pace. Why even be given a gas pedal and a siren with lights if you weren't willing to go a hundred miles an hour when you needed to?

Damned pansy-ass driver.

After an eternity or seven, they pulled up to the ER and Stu told him gruffly to stay the hell outta the way while they unloaded Brooklyn. Elijah nodded and, reluctantly letting go of her hand, shrunk himself as small as he could go into the corner. Whatever it took, that's what he'd do.

They unloaded the gurney and wheeled it through the ER doors, with Nurse Knutsen and Doctor Torgeson already there, ready to take over. "Is she allergic to anything?" Dr. Torgeson hollered at him.

Elijah shook his head. "Nothing," he said.

"Good." They were pushing the cart back through some swinging double doors and Eli went to follow 'em when the nurse shouted back at him, "You stay in the waiting room. Get your paperwork filled out."

Elijah stopped and stared after them, watching until they turned the corner and disappeared from sight.

*Please God, please God, please God…*

There wasn't anything else left for him to do.

Again.

# CHAPTER 36

## HANNAH

S HE RAN THE CURRY BRUSH over the mahogany flanks of Wildflower, shining in the early morning light. Many teachers spent their summers far away from where they worked, taking full advantage of being footloose and fancy free for three whole months, but Hannah stayed right there in Sawyer. Summers for her meant lots of time on horseback, lots of time weeding the garden, and this summer, lots of time crying.

Not this morning, though. Why, it was almost seven o'clock and she hadn't cried even once. That was pretty good, right?

She stroked down the flanks of her gorgeous mare – and momma to Wild Rose – talking softly as she went. "I know you miss Dad," she said as Wildflower snuffled in her hair, giving her a horsey kiss. "I'd take you to the center but somehow, I don't think they want a horse there, pooping everywhere, even one as pretty as you." Wildflower nickered softly at that, and Hannah chuckled. "You know you're pretty, and that's the problem. You don't have to behave because you—"

Her cell phone began vibrating in her pocket.

She frowned, shoving the handle of the curry brush into her back pocket even as she pulled her cell phone out. A number was flashing on the screen that she didn't recognize, but it was local, so she swiped to answer. "Hello, Hannah Lambert speaking," she said formally, just as her parents had taught her to do when she was a small child.

"Miss Lambert, it's Officer Morland from the Long Valley County Sheriff's Office."

"Of course. How are you?" she asked politely, even as panic started to creep up her spine. Hannah and Aaron graduated from high school together. She darn well knew who the man was. He didn't need to introduce himself like they hadn't spent twelve years of their lives sitting in the same classroom as each other.

So the fact that he was…

A whole-body shiver ran over her and she clung to the phone, hoping against hope that this was going to be a phone call with good news, and Aaron was introducing himself as a county cop because…

Even her fevered imagination couldn't come up with a good reason for it, and that definitely wasn't a good sign.

All formality disappeared as soon as Aaron started talking. "Sarah Morland was in a car wreck last night, a little after three in the morning. Drunk as a skunk, with Brooklyn in the backseat of the Escalade."

Which was when the world disappeared down a long tunnel.

"Wha…" she said weakly, leaning against the flanks of Wildflower. Just like the day the principal had talked to her, the world started to go dark around the edges and Hannah was sure her knees were going to give out.

Still in cop mode, Aaron kept going. "Sarah is in jail, sleeping it off. Elijah is here at the hospital with Brooklyn. She's got a broken leg and they think she has a ruptured spleen. They've done a CT scan and she has internal bleeding. They're doing emergency surgery now. They're hoping to only take part of the spleen, depending on the damage, so we'll see what happens when they're done. Elijah—" Aaron let out a heavy sigh. "My idiotic brother thinks that I shouldn't be calling you 'cause of what happened at the school, but I told him to stop being a dumbass and call you. He wouldn't, so I did. You better get your ass down here, Hannah. My brother needs you, and so does Brooklyn."

"Of course," Hannah said mechanically, already pushing her body to move towards the house, closing the horse stall and barn door behind her as she went. She could hear Wildflower and Wild Rose nickering behind her, wanting to know why she hadn't given them their oats yet, but she ignored them. No matter what they thought, they wouldn't actually die if they didn't get their oats today.

*But Brooklyn might die today.*

Hannah shoved the tears down. She could have a mental breakdown later.

"I'm on my way now," she promised, and hung up. She was wearing her old cowboy boots, covered in horse manure and straw, and her holey jeans she wore when she was cleaning out the stalls, oh, and she hadn't bothered to put in her contacts that morning, but none of that mattered.

Not right now.

It wasn't until she slid into her car that she realized she still had the curry brush sticking out of her back pocket. Even as she threw her car into reverse, she wiggled the brush out and tossed it into the passenger seat. She tore through town as fast as she dared, wishing that she had a light she could throw on top of her car that'd allow her to bust through the only stoplight in town without slowing down.

"Please God, please God, please God," she chanted as she took a corner stupidly fast, hearing her tires squeal as she went. The cautious Hannah inside of her was terrified by the speeds she was driving inside the city limits of Sawyer, but she told Cautious Hannah to go fly a kite. "Brooklyn needs you," she said aloud. "And Elijah too."

After the world's longest drive going approximately a thousand miles an hour or so, Hannah screeched to a stop outside of the Long Valley County Hospital and took off at a run towards the sliding ER doors, horse manure flying as her legs went pumping.

*Please God, please God, please God.*

Nurse Knutsen looked up when Hannah came tearing through the front door, weary and tired from her overnight shift. "Hey, Hannah," she said, doing her best to be friendly despite her exhaustion. "Elijah is back through the doors and to the right."

Hannah nodded her thanks as she sprinted past. The janitorial staff were probably going to wonder why there was poop and mud everywhere when they cleaned, but Hannah just couldn't find it in herself to care at that moment. Nothing mattered but Elijah and Brooklyn.

When she saw Elijah, pacing back and forth like a caged animal, she ran straight at him, not giving a good gosh darn about who saw or what they said.

"Elijah!" she cried as she threw her arms around him. He stiffened up in shock. "I can't believe...how is she?"

Elijah's arms came down around her slowly as he stared, his mouth gaping open. "How did you...why are you here?" he sputtered.

"Aaron called and told me what happened. Is Brooklyn still in surgery?" she demanded impatiently. Forget why she was there – she needed some answers, and she needed them yesterday.

"Yeah. No one's come out yet to tell me what's going on, so I'm guessing they're still working on her. Why are you here?!" he repeated, still stiff with shock.

She laughed a little, tears of relief from being in his arms starting to roll down her cheeks. Even with Brooklyn in surgery, the world felt a little more...right just standing there, Elijah as her rock. "Brooklyn was in a car wreck," she said in her best 'duh' voice. "Do you really think I'd stay away?"

The corners of Elijah's mouth quirked up a little at that. "You're a sight better momma than Sarah ever could be," he whispered, brushing the tendrils back from her face that had escaped from her braid. "If she had half the love for Brooksy that you did…well, we wouldn't be here in this hospital right now, would we?"

Hannah shook her head. "Sarah's loss," she told him bluntly. "I hate to question your taste in women, since you seem to like me all right, but Sarah is one heck of a mess. She needs…well, a lot of things, but mostly she needs to not be drinking every night." *And morning and afternoon.*

She took a deep breath. It was easy to point out everything that Sarah needed to fix, but quite another to acknowledge her own mistakes. She was slowly – ever so slowly – learning how to pull on her big girl panties every morning, and it was time for her to do it again.

"Elijah, I've been thinking," she announced firmly, looking him in the eye as she said it. He looked startled by her forcefulness.

"Yeah?"

"Yeah. You need to go to school to become an electrician."

If he looked startled before, he looked dumbfounded now. "A…a…an electrician? Are you being serious right now?"

"Of course I'm being serious. And if you tell me that you're too stupid to be an electrician, I just might hit you over the head and you'd deserve it, too."

His mouth snapped closed.

"You have skills with these hands of yours, and I don't just mean…you know." She felt the blood rush into her cheeks as she waved her hands in the general direction of her body. She glanced guiltily around the hospital waiting room for surgical patients, hoping no one could overhear her, but the only other person in the room had his earbuds in and was playing on his phone, so they were probably safe.

"You fixed my ballast when I didn't even know what a ballast was. And then you rewired the light for Mrs. Croft when it kept blowing every light bulb she put into it. And you switched the wires around in the cafeteria so the light switch on the wall actually flips up to turn on, and flips down to turn off. Principal Zeller heard it from almost everyone at the school when he fired you – one teacher said she didn't care if you howled under the full moon buck-naked every month, you were actually doing your job and she wanted you back. But you shouldn't go back. You need to go to school, just not the Cleveland Elementary School."

She finally ran out of words and so she shut up and waited to hear all of his excuses – maybe about his parents telling him he was too stupid to do it, or how he—

"I can't afford to," he said simply. "College students go to school and live in dorm rooms and eat ramen noodle and drink lots of cheap beer and their parents lend 'em $20 when they need to do laundry. That's not an option for me. I've got a kid who needs me, 'specially now that her momma is in jail and is probably gonna stay there—"

Which was when Hannah did the bravest thing she ever did in her whole life, pulling her big girl panties up so high, they were threatening to end up around her ears.

"Elijah Morland, will you marry me?"

# CHAPTER 37

## ELIJAH

E LIJAH WAS GONNA need dental work after how hard his jaw hit the floor at that one.

"You…you wanna marry me?" he asked, wanting to make sure he was understanding her. Maybe he got into the car wreck along with Brooksy, and now he was having delusions or something.

"More than anything." She was staring straight at him, not blinking, not hemming or hawing around. His mind flashed back to high school, when he'd been a freshman and she'd been a senior. She'd been so quiet then, he wasn't sure if he'd even heard her talk that whole year.

And now? His chest filled with pride at how much she'd changed and grown over the past year. She wasn't anything like the Hannah she used to be, and he was damn proud of her for that.

That didn't make what she was saying a good idea, though. No matter how much he wanted it, it just wasn't fair to stick someone as smart and talented as Hannah with a dumbo like him. It was only right for him to shut this idea down, right here, right now.

"Hannah, we aren't…we shouldn't…I mean…"

He shut his mouth and rubbed at his jaw, before he stuck his boot so far down his throat, it came out his asshole. Truth time: No matter what he was *supposed* to do, it was killing him to say the words, and he was afraid she'd actually listen to what was coming outta his mouth and not wanna marry him after all.

"Darling, I wanna marry you," he tried again. "I've been wanting to for months now. But you seem to think that marrying you will solve the problem of me not having the money to go to school, and that just plain isn't true. You're a teacher, for God's sakes. You aren't exactly rolling in the dough yourself."

"No, I'm not," she agreed with a laugh, stroking light fingers down his face, staring up at him. Her big blue eyes were all distorted behind her thick glasses, but he realized in that moment that she was more beautiful to him than ever before. Her soul was what made her beautiful, and Hannah had the prettiest soul of 'em all.

"But, I told you before – we're better together. I don't have a house payment or rent or anything. I only owe property taxes on my home; otherwise, it's mine. Plus, we're both paying utility bills right now – if we're married and are living together, then we have half the utility bills that we had before. Also – and I doubt you've thought this far ahead – I really don't think you'll be paying child support after this. Sarah is going to be cooling her heels in jail for a good long while. Even our illustrious judge of Long Valley County will have a hard time overlooking the fact that she came this close," she held up her thumb and forefinger, "to killing Brooklyn."

They stopped and stared at each other, the reality of that last statement making Elijah want to puke into the nearest trash can.

"Sorry, I didn't mean to sound flip about that," Hannah said, looking a little green around the gills herself. "That came out all wrong. You know how much I love Brooklyn. But I can't imagine that even Judge Schmidt would be able to ignore what a terrible mother Sarah is, you know?"

"God, I hope not," Elijah said, pulling Hannah against his chest and running his hands down her back. "You're right – I hadn't thought about that. My brain just keeps going 'round and 'round – what if she isn't okay? Surgery is scary, and anything at all could go wrong. But the other thing I can't believe is how you knew..." He trailed off, the lump in his throat making it hard for him to talk.

"Knew what?" she asked, pulling back to look up at him.

"Knew that I wanted to be an electrician," he whispered, pulling her back against his chest. Having her in his arms just felt right, and he didn't want to let her go, not even so she could look up at him. "All my life, I wanted to. When I was gonna go to get some schooling after high school, that's what I was gonna become. And then Sarah...well anyway, I didn't tell you that 'cause I thought I was being stupid to want it. That I'm not good enough or smart enough. I can't believe you figured out my dream when I was too much of a scaredy cat to tell you what it was."

She tilted just her head back, staying snuggled against him as she ran her fingers through his hair. "It just seems right. It's what you're meant to be. Elijah the Electrician. It has a real nice ring to it." She went up on her toes and pressed her mouth to his. "You'll be the best electrician this town has ever seen, I'm sure of it."

"What about the school district?" Elijah asked skeptically. "What's Mr. Zeller gonna say about you and I getting hitched?"

Her face went a little white, but she stood firm. "They're not going to be happy. They'll probably see this as me thumbing my nose at them, and maybe I am. But a lot of their worry about us dating was the blowback from Sarah, and the lawsuits she was going to file. With Sarah driving drunk and putting Brooklyn's life in danger like she did, I don't think she'll want to go looking for another fight. And even if the school board is angry with me for marrying you, well...I don't give a good gosh darn. Even Principal Zeller said they can't tell me who I can date outside of school. I dare them to take me on. I'll fight them tooth and nail."

Elijah laughed disbelievingly. "I don't know where this Hannah came from, but I'm not gonna question it. I'm so damn proud of you. I couldn't—"

"Mr. Morland?"

They both turned to see the doctor in the doorway, a tired but pleased smile on his face.

"Your daughter is coming out of surgery now," Dr. Torgeson said, "but I wanted to let you know how it went. Terrific, honestly. It couldn't have gone better. I only had to take a small portion of her spleen – less than 10%, and as young as she is, she's gonna heal up right quick. We found nothing else while we were in there. You want to go see her?"

Wanna go see her? Elijah felt like someone had just asked him if he wanted to win a million dollars. Of course he wanted to go see her. "Yes, sir!" he said, grabbing Hannah's hand and dragging her down the hallway after him.

*She's okay. She's okay. She's gonna be just fine. She's okay.*

The 1-ton bull that'd been sitting on his chest finally moved a little, letting Elijah breathe just a bit better.

Dr. Torgeson pulled the curtain back and let 'em in to see Brooksy lying there, sleeping like an angel – well, an angel with tubes going every which way.

Together, they hurried to her side, Hannah asking as they went about hot water and wash rags to clean her up.

"Of course," the doctor said, nodding towards the teenage gal in the candy striper outfit in the corner. "We were so focused on stopping the internal bleeding, we didn't pay attention to anything else."

As the teen hurried off to get the stuff, Hannah and Elijah stepped to either side of the bed, not talking, but simply moving as a team.

"Brooksy, you awake?" Elijah whispered, taking her limp hand and squeezing it. She was so little and pale, like she didn't have a drop of blood left in her, and even as the doctor went over what to expect and how well the surgery went, Eli couldn't help but think the doctor got it all wrong. Just looking at his daughter, usually so full of energy that she pert near vibrated with it, and now she was just lying still as a stone, not moving a bit...that wasn't right. That wasn't his Brooksy.

Finally, some movement – Brooksy moaned as she tossed her head on the pillow. Elijah wanted to drop to his knees to thank God for it.

"Hey, darling, how are you feeling?" Hannah asked quietly, wiping some of the dried mud from Brooksy's face. "I bet your side is really hurting, isn't it?"

Brooksy nodded, her eyes still closed, and squeezed Hannah's hand a little. "Thirsty," she whispered.

Hannah looked up at the candy striper who'd come back with the wash clothes and water. "Water in a cup with a straw, please," she said crisply, like she was used to taking care of people in hospital beds. She had it a lot more together than Elijah did, that was for damn sure. He was so happy that Brooksy was alive and speaking, all he wanted to do was let some tears out from sheer relief.

Brooksy struggled to open her eyes. "You came to see me," she whispered, looking up at Hannah. "I thought you didn't like me no more."

"Oh, Brooklyn," Hannah said, her voice quivering, "your mom was just so upset with me and how I helped you get ready in the morning...it was causing a lot of problems at the school. But I love you so very much, and being away from you was making my heart hurt." She picked up Brooksy's hand and held it against her chest. "I'm sorry I couldn't see you."

Before Elijah could talk himself out of it, before he could tell himself not to do it, he opened up his mouth. "I know something that's gonna make you feel better," he said, keeping his eyes glued to Brooksy even as he felt, more than saw,

Hannah stiffen up beside him. "Miss Lambert and I are gonna get married."

Hannah let out a little startled gasp, and Brooksy, struggling to concentrate through the medicine, looked dazedly between them.

"For realsies?" she whispered, her voice all scratchy. "You're not teasing me, right, Dad?"

"I'd never tease you about something this important," Elijah said, squeezing her hand. He looked across the hospital bed to Hannah, who had her hand up over her mouth, her eyes welling with tears. She reached her hand out to him, holding onto Brooksy's with her other hand. They made a daisy chain, the three of them.

"I was thinking," Hannah said, looking back down at Brooksy, "that you better heal pretty quick, because I need a flower girl who knows what she's doing, and I figured you were just the person to ask."

"Flower girl? Really?" Brooksy grinned a grin as big as the moon. "I'll be the best flower girl ever," she promised as her eyes started fluttering shut. "Can my dress be pink?"

"The biggest, floofiest, pinkest dress you ever did see," Hannah promised her. "You go to sleep so you can wake up better, okay?"

"Okay," Brooksy whispered, and then she was gone again, drifting on a cloud of painkillers.

"She didn't ask about Sarah," Hannah said, looking at him, worrying her bottom lip with her teeth. "Not even to know if she had been hurt or killed or anything."

Elijah pulled her hand up to his lips and kissed her knuckles. "She was pretty far under with all of the drugs and everything. She'll probably be awake enough next time to think to ask. But she already told you – you're her momma. I know my baby girl – that's not gonna change."

The tears that'd been threatening took a spill down her cheeks, and Hannah swiped at them, embarrassed. "I didn't even put my contacts in this morning," she said with a little laugh. "Are you sure you want to marry a bug-eyed girl like me?"

"I've never been more sure of anything in my whole life," he said seriously. "I don't deserve you, but I know that, and I'll do my best not to screw this up. If I ever stick my foot so far down my throat that you can find it coming out my ass, you just tell me. I'll try. I'll try real hard, but I'm not perfect."

"That's good," Hannah said, teasing him. The glint in her eye said it all. "If you were, you wouldn't want me anyway."

"Hush your crazy talk and come on over and kiss me. I've missed you something fierce."

As she hurried around the end of the bed and settled down on his lap to give him a kiss he was sure he'd never forget, he swore to himself that he'd never go without his Hannah again. Life just weren't worth living without her, and if she was happy with him, who was he to talk her outta loving him? Some things, a man just shouldn't question.

# EPILOGUE

## HANNAH

December, 2019

ICHELLE AND CARLA grinned at her in matching bright purple dresses, the halter-neck style making both of them look like a million bucks.

"Thanks for everything, you guys," Hannah said tearfully, dabbing carefully at the corners of her eyes. After all of the hard work that Carla had done on her makeup, she couldn't cry it all away. "I can't believe I'm the first one to leave our little club. Who's going to be the secretary of the Early Spinster's Club now?"

"It's your wedding day," Michelle said bluntly. "You've got better things to worry about. Like how handsome that man of yours is lookin', out in the chapel, waiting for you up at the altar."

Hannah carefully hugged Michelle, and then Carla. "You're right, but...this never would've happened without you two. Thank you both for forcing me to be braver than I ever thought I could be."

"Momma," Brooklyn whispered, sticking her head around the door, "Dad is waiting for you up at the altar and he looks nervous. You better hurry up the aisle before he pukes." She disappeared, her seventy yards of brilliant sparkling pink fabric taking a lot longer to exit the room.

"That dress," Michelle whispered, horrified.

"I know, right?!" Carla exclaimed, clearly jealous. "I bet she feels like a fairy princess in it."

Actually, Hannah had only just barely managed to keep Brooklyn from pinning wings to the back of it. She was going to wear that dress until it had to be peeled off her in strips, she was sure of it. Hannah wasn't much of a froufrou sort of person, so to her, the dress just looked like a mix between whipped cream and Pepto Bismol with a dash of glitter for funsies, but it made Brooklyn happy and that was all that mattered.

The other part she'd had to put her foot down and count to three on was Brooklyn's choice in shoes. She'd wanted Sunday shoes with heels on them, but Hannah had said absolutely not. Brooklyn's leg was all healed up and the cast was off, but Hannah wasn't willing to take a chance on her breaking her leg again on the walk up the center aisle. So Brooklyn had settled on a pair of glittering gold slippers that matched Hannah's, instead.

Carla picked up the oversized bridal bouquet, filled with every flower under the sun, and thrust it into her hands. "You're gonna do great," she said, dashing away a stray tear of her own. "Just remember…Marewage," she said in her best *Princess-Bride* impersonation. "Marewage is what brings us togeder to-day."

Hannah laughed as she hugged Carla one last time. Of course Carla was quoting *Princess Bride*. It was her all-time favorite movie. Heck, Carla could probably quote every line in it from start to finish. "I can't wait until your wedding day," she teased Carla. "I'm going to quote every line from *Princess Bride* to you that I can remember." Which was considerably less than all that Carla had memorized, but she'd study up before the big day, just to be sure she did a bang-up job of it.

And then somehow, she was walking down the aisle, Brooklyn in front of her, gracefully tossing flower petals with all of the gravity and seriousness her eleven-year-old soul could muster. Hannah looked up and caught eyes with Elijah. For once, he wasn't watching his daughter like a hawk to make sure that nothing bad was happening to her; his eyes were pinned on Hannah. He didn't blink, he didn't look away; she wondered if he even breathed. He just watched her, his eyes saying all that his actions over the past 18 months had said without words:

*I love you, Hannah-soon-to-be-Morland. I love you more than I love the sun, the moon, and the stars. I'm sorry your papa couldn't walk you down the aisle. I'm proud of you for choosing to walk down it by yourself instead. You're the bravest woman I know, and even if I don't deserve you, I will always love you.*

Hannah made her way up to the front, Michelle and Carla standing on the left side of the platform, with Brooklyn on the right, standing next to Aaron who was serving as Elijah's best man.

Their parents, unhappy about what a scandal the two of them had caused by dating even after the school district had fired Elijah, hadn't been invited to the wedding. Hannah's mother was watching from heaven, while her father...

Well, the father she'd known and loved growing up would've loved to have been there for his only child, and that was the father she clung to in her mind.

Sarah couldn't be there for the big day, what with her being in jail for the next five to seven years, depending on her good behavior behind bars. Hannah could only hope she got the help she needed for her alcohol dependency while she was incarcerated.

When she made it up to the front of the chapel, Elijah slipped his arm through hers, steadying her, as they looked up at the pastor. Hannah clasped her bouquet to her, holding on for dear life.

*Speaking of life...*

It was more of a rollercoaster; more of an adventure; more of a thrill ride than the old Hannah ever would've known, but with Elijah and Brooklyn by her side, she was ready to take any of it on, and more.

∪ ∪ ∪

QUICK AUTHOR'S NOTE

I CONCEIVED of Hannah's storyline many moons ago, while I was writing Sugar and Jaxson's love story in *Flames of Love*. Richard Schmidt was just such an asshole, as was his father, that it seemed like he'd affect more than one person's life in a negative way.

(Not to give it all away, but Richard Schmidt, aka Dickwad, will be showing up in a future novel, too. I won't say anything more than that here. #TotalTease)

And like all good plot lines that I write, Elijah's story was also based on reality. My handsome hubby's uncle went through a nasty custodial battle with the mother of his daughter, and he got a job at the school as a janitor simply so he could still see his daughter every day. That's the kind of love every father should have for their children, and wouldn't we be a better world for it if that was true?

One last thought: I dedicated this book to my own Hannah, one of my closest friends in the world, and a person who also happens to be one of the best teachers your child could ever be blessed with. I borrowed some traits of hers while writing this story to make it more real; others, I made up wholesale. But the struggle of being a teacher and living on low, almost poverty wages, is a very real one for her and millions of other teachers across the US. *Time Magazine* did an in-depth article on this topic in 2018 that you can find online if you'd like.

Looking forward, there are many more stories still to come in the world of Long Valley. Michelle's story will be in *Sheltered by Love* which I don't have a go-live date for yet, but Carla's story has already gone live; it's the 10th novel in the Cowboys of Long Valley Romance series, *Bloom of Love*.

Oh, and Aaron Morland is coming too – I haven't found just the right girl to bring him to heel yet, so his story is hanging out in the to-be-announced section. :)

But in the meanwhile, the next book in this series is *Baked with Love*, when the hunka-hunka love, Gage Dyer and baker extraordinaire, finally finds love of his own, but not before going through a hell of wringer. You'll just have to read it to find out, but the whole "Richard Schmidt shows up in a later book" thing? Yeah, this is the book where that happens.

It is available at your favorite book retailer or local library, so be sure to find it there for the chance to see Gage meet his match…

Thank you to everyone for all of your love and support – it's such a cheesy saying but it's true: I couldn't do this without you. Thank you for helping me make my dreams come true.

*Erin Wright*

*Be sure to find my books at your favorite bookstore, retailer, or library*

*Or, buy them directly from me at*
**https://ErinWright.net/My-Books**

*If you prefer, you can also scan this QR code with your phone:*

# ALSO BY ERIN WRIGHT

## ~ COWBOYS OF LONG VALLEY ROMANCE ~

*Accounting for Love*

*Blizzard of Love*

*Arrested by Love*

*Returning for Love*

*Christmas of Love*

*Overdue for Love*

*Bundle of Love*

*Lessons in Love*

*Baked with Love*

*Bloom of Love*

*Broken by Love* (TBA)

*Holly and Love* (TBA)

*Banking on Love* (TBA)

*Sheltered by Love* (TBA)

## ~ FIREFIGHTERS OF LONG VALLEY ROMANCE ~

*Flames of Love*

*Inferno of Love*

*Fire and Love*

*Burned by Love*

~ MUSICIANS OF LONG VALLEY ROMANCE ~

*Strummin' Up Love*

*Melody of Love* (TBA)

*Rock 'N Love* (TBA)

*Rhapsody of Love* (TBA)


~ SERVICEMEN OF LONG VALLEY ROMANCE ~

*Thankful for Love* (TBA)

*Commanded to Love* (TBA)

*Salute to Love* (TBA)

*Harbored by Love* (TBA)

# About Erin Wright

USA Today Bestselling author Erin Wright has worked every job under the sun, including library director, barista, teacher, website designer, and ranch hand helping brand cattle, before settling into the career she's always dreamed about: Author.

She still loves coffee, doesn't love the smell of cow flesh burning, and is currently living out her own love story in a tiny town in rural Idaho.

*Wanna get in touch?*
https://erinwright.net
erin@erinwright.net

*Or reach out to Erin on your favorite social media platform:*

facebook.com/AuthorErinWright
x.com/ErinWrightLV
youtube.com/@ErinWrightLV
pinterest.com/ErinWrightBooks
goodreads.com/ErinWright
bookbub.com/profile/Erin-Wright
instagram.com/AuthorErinWright

www.ingramcontent.com/pod-product-compliance
Lightning Source LLC
Chambersburg PA
CBHW070631170726
48291CB00003B/969